M000012450

Praise for
New York Times and USA Today Bestselling Author
Diane Capri

"Full of thrills and tension, but smart and human, too."
Lee Child, #1 World Wide Bestselling Author of Jack Reacher
Thrillers

"[A] welcome surprise....[W]orks from the first page
to 'The End'."
Larry King

"Swift pacing and ongoing suspense are always
present...[L]ikable protagonist who uses her political
connections for a good cause...Readers should eagerly anticipate
the next [book]."
Top Pick, Romantic Times

"...offers tense legal drama with courtroom overtones, twisty
plot, and loads of Florida atmosphere. Recommended."
Library Journal

"[A] fast-paced legal thriller...energetic prose...an appealing
heroine...clever and capable supporting cast...[that will] keep
readers waiting for the next [book]."
Publishers Weekly

"Expertise shines on every page."
Margaret Maron, Edgar, Anthony, Agatha and Macavity Award
Winning MWA Past President

EARLY
CHECK OUT

by DIANE CAPRI

Copyright © 2019 Diane Capri, LLC
All Rights Reserved

All rights reserved as permitted under the U.S. Copyright Act of 1976. No part of the publication may be reproduced, distributed, or transmitted in any form or by any means, or stored in a database or retrieval system, without the prior permission of the publisher. The only exception is brief quotation in printed reviews.

Published by: AugustBooks
http://www.AugustBooks.com

ISBN: 978-1-942633-27-3

Original cover design by: Dar Albert
Digital formatting by: Author E.M.S.
Interior cat silhouettes used under CC0 license from openclipart.org.

Early Check Out is a work of fiction. Names, characters, places, and incidents either are the product of the author's imagination or are used fictitiously, and any resemblance to actual persons, living or dead, business establishments, events, or locales is entirely coincidental.

Published in the United States of America.

Visit the author website:
http://www.DianeCapri.com

ALSO BY DIANE CAPRI

The Park Hotel Mysteries Series
Reservation with Death
Early Check Out
Room with a Clue
Late Arrival

The Hunt for Justice Series
Due Justice
Twisted Justice
Secret Justice
Wasted Justice
Raw Justice
Mistaken Justice (*novella*)
Cold Justice (*novella*)
False Justice (*novella*)
Fair Justice (*novella*)
True Justice (*novella*)
Night Justice

The Heir Hunter Series
Blood Trails
Trace Evidence

Jordan Fox Mysteries Series
False Truth
(An 11-book continuity series)

The Hunt for Jack Reacher Series:

The Jess Kimball Thrillers Series

EARLY
CHECK OUT

CHAPTER ONE

Dear Miss Charlotte,

As promised, I'm writing again to update you on my last week or so at the Park Hotel. I'm the concierge here now, my new job! I'm settling in nicely, and folks are starting to accept me as a "regular" fixture—almost. These things take time, I know, and it has been quite a change for all of us. But I'm feeling hopeful and positive these days.

I wish you could come for a visit. I know you'd love Frontenac Island as much as I do. Everything is so green and cheerful. The breeze off the lake is refreshing, and sometimes I just walk out onto the bluff and stare off across Lake Michigan. It's so relaxing here.

I've met some of the most down-to-earth and charming people so far. Some folks are downright colorful and entertaining—I could tell you endless stories about JC and Reggie, the two old men who play chess down at the docks. Or the guys who own the soap shop in town—they make a lot of gift baskets and such for the hotel. I know you'd love Ginny, of course, and would probably get along well with her mother, Lois, who runs the hotel. She has your sensibilities and your work ethic, for sure.

Yes, I did hear from my mother. Of course, I told them I'd moved. They want me to come to Hong Kong, which I'm sure you've already guessed. I haven't had a chance to connect with them yet, mostly because I've been so busy and the time difference makes things difficult. But don't worry. I'm not moving halfway around the world!

Not everyone is pleased with me being here, especially not Ginny's grandpa, Samuel, but you know me—I don't let him bully me around. I plan on making this concierge gig work out. You always taught me to do my best no matter what. So, with your voice in my head, I'm putting everything I have into this job.

Oh, things got a little crazy here during my first week. You might have caught it on the news—but just in case you haven't heard, I'm enclosing a few clippings from the local newspaper, so you can read the details for yourself. That's mostly the reason Samuel is not so thrilled with me. He thinks I'll ruin his hotel by sticking my nose into things I shouldn't.

That's all over and done with now, thank goodness. I hadn't planned to get involved, but you know I can't just sit back and do nothing when I can help. Still, I'm going to steer clear of trouble from now on. I've had enough to last me a lifetime. Let's hope "trouble" leaves me alone! Ha ha.

I miss you, Miss Charlotte. Take care of all those nieces and nephews. They don't know how lucky they are to have you bossing them around. They'll be fine ladies and gentlemen one day because of you. I'm sure of it.

Oh! I have a business card now, and it's also enclosed. I hope to hear from you soon.

All my love,

Andi

CHAPTER TWO

I READ THE LETTER ONE last time, signed with a flourish, sealed the envelope and put a stamp on it. I'd drop it in the mailbox in the lobby. Writing to Miss Charlotte regularly kept her from worrying so much about me. The last thing I wanted was to worry Miss Charlotte. Which meant I didn't tell her everything, the way I'd done when I was a kid. What she didn't know couldn't worry her, right?

So I downplayed the issues with my parents, which I'd been ignoring, and the problems I'd been having with Samuel Park, among other things. At that point, I didn't even know I was going to find another body, but I certainly wouldn't have mentioned *that* to Miss Charlotte, anyway.

For the past few days, I'd done my best to prove to Samuel, Ginny's grandpa and owner of the Park Hotel, that I was suited to be the concierge. After his unexpected arrival at the family dinner—when he declared that his hotel was going down the crapper and I was somehow responsible for it—he'd been putting me through my paces.

Every single day, he told me several times, "Guests are kings at the Park Hotel, Andi." Like he'd ever give me a chance to forget that, anyway.

He challenged me at every turn with outlandish tasks like filling an entire suite with balloon animals for a birthday party or organizing a wedding proposal with two goats as the bearers of the flowers and the engagement ring. He insisted that an excellent concierge should be able to handle any request as long as it wasn't illegal, immoral, or impossible. "The Park Hotel offers extraordinary service, Andi. First, last, and always."

I agreed, in theory. But I suspected that these particular requests didn't actually come from guests but from Samuel's box of one thousand fun ways to run me out of the Park Hotel.

On a daily basis, he told me that Casey Cushing, the former concierge, had been able to accomplish virtually anything, and without a single issue or complaint. He said Casey could do twice the work in less time. That Casey never asked for a single day off.

So far, Samuel hadn't claimed that Casey Cushing could leap tall buildings in a single bound or was faster than a speeding bullet, but I figured those claims were coming. Maybe he was saving them for an upcoming round of attempting to make me feel weak and useless, as well as unwelcome at the Park.

I didn't understand his constant barrage of "Casey is amazing" anecdotes until I found out that he and Casey's mom—who'd undergone hip surgery recently—were old friends. When Ginny had told me, she'd rolled her eyes, so I assumed that meant maybe they were more than friends. Talk about robbing the cradle, though. I mean, Samuel was in his late seventies at least. And considering Casey's age, his mom couldn't be any older than early fifties.

Oh, and I also found out that Samuel had hired Casey to begin with. Of course he'd think Casey was the best thing since avocado toast.

Talk about pressure. How could I ever measure up to the amazing Casey? But I planned to give it my best.

So, this was what I was dealing with on top of the regular duties I'd been assigned, like replicating the meal a couple had on their wedding day fifty years ago so it could be served at the anniversary party. It didn't matter that the chef who had prepared the meal was long dead and no one working in the Park's kitchen had any kind of clue how to cook like he had. I made several uncomfortable phone calls only to find out that some of his recipes had been lost with him.

"So, do you think you could replicate all of his dishes?" I asked the head chef as we powwowed in the small, cramped back office which belonged to Nicole, who managed the restaurant.

Justin glanced at the newly created menu I'd handed him. "Yeah, seems pretty basic. Nothing too fancy. Dover sole almandine sounds a lot more difficult than it actually is."

"These are the notes I was able to gather from a few people who attended the wedding fifty years ago about the meal." I handed him three pages of handwritten notes.

His eyebrows came up at that. "Wow, impressive work, Andi."

"Yeah, I had to make a lot of phone calls for those."

"A bit much, don't you think?"

"Not according to the big boss, it isn't."

Justin chuckled. "I've had a couple of impromptu inspections from Samuel myself since he's been back.

Fortunately for me, he can't even boil water, so he thinks what I do is some kind of magic."

"Which it is. But he's very sly," I said. "He looks like this kindly old man with a warm inviting grin, but really, he's this tyrant with judgment in his icy-blue stare. I can't do anything right as far as he's concerned."

"I agree, but I'd be careful who you say that around," Justin cautioned in hushed tones as he glanced pointedly toward Nicole's closed office door.

"Oh, I know. I'm quickly learning who's on my side…"

The door to the office opened, and Nicole walked in. She stopped short and looked at us both. Speaking of judgment. It radiated off her like nuclear waste.

"What's going on?" she asked.

"Andi was just filling me in on the menu request for the big fiftieth wedding anniversary celebration we're hosting at the hotel next week." He held up the menu as evidence. "I'll get right on it, Andi. Thanks." And he left. Smart move.

I wasn't able to extract myself as easily. Nicole was worse than Samuel. She was constantly looking for ways to make me look bad. Not sure why she disliked me so much. It had to be more than just the fact that her husband and I had a brief fling back when I was in college. Not really even a fling. Just one casual date. We'd maybe kissed once, and it hadn't been earth shattering or anything, because I didn't even remember the kiss, if there'd been one.

I'd been tempted to ask Nicole about her attitude toward me on a couple of occasions but always chickened out—especially when she gave me the disparaging look she was giving me right at the moment.

"Shouldn't you be getting back to your…desk?" She said it like "desk" was one of those filthy four-letter words.

"Nope. I'm actually off the clock. Just had to talk to Justin about the menu."

"Oh."

"Always a pleasure, Nicole." I flipped around and walked out of the little space, through the bustling kitchen, through the restaurant, and into the lobby of the hotel.

I looked out the big bay windows and smiled. It was a gorgeous sunny day with a sky as blue as a robin's egg, *and* I had time off. Time off that didn't include recuperating from the chaos of a murder investigation. One I'd essentially solved, although the sheriff would never, ever admit to that fact. I'd barely received a thank-you from the guy, even after I thought we had reached a turning point in our, uh…in our association.

Since it was such a beautiful day, I decided to walk down the big hill to the village and check on my cats, Scout and Jem, at Daisy's Pet Hotel. Yes, that was a thing on the island. It was actually pretty cool, and I really liked the owner, Daisy.

For the first week on the island, I was able to keep my feline family in my suite, but Lois insisted I find alternative arrangements for them. The hotel had a strict "no pets" policy, and that rule was also enforced with the live-in staff. Ginny had tried to talk her mother around, insisting that Scout and Jem were like my babies, but Lois put her foot down. Actually, she kept it down like it was glued to the floor. Sometimes that woman was hard as nails.

We probably would've had a better chance of persuading her if Samuel hadn't shown up. I was pretty sure Lois's father-in-law ran her ragged—even worse than he ran me—questioning everything with the same sour scowl.

Poor Lois. I felt for her. I definitely wouldn't want to be walking in her shoes right now, though my position was a lot more precarious than hers. She was actual family, after all, and I was not. Hell, she was the one who owned the place since her husband, Henry, had died. Samuel couldn't actually throw her out on the street like he could do to me.

I was just about to head out the front doors when someone called after me. I recognized the voice. Samuel Park. Ugh! "Hey, Andi. Hold up."

I considered ignoring the voice, pretending like I didn't hear it. But that would've been career suicide at this juncture. I needed this job because nothing had changed regarding my license to practice law, which was still submerged under the dark cloud of suspicion. I couldn't work as a lawyer anywhere right now. Not while my former boss, Jeremy, was running from the law. He was guilty of embezzlement, for sure. But I was being judged guilty by mere association.

I turned with a wide, bright smile on my face. "Hello, Samuel."

He was a handsome man. A full head of silver hair and a sharp dresser. Every woman of a certain age would be proud to have him escort her anywhere. As always, he looked at me with icy-blue eyes through his perpetual frown. "Are you going into the village today?"

"Actually, I am."

"Good." He thrust a big envelope into my hands. "Drop this off to June Biddle." He eyed me and issued yet another of his unending challenges. "You do know who June is, don't you?

"Yes, of course I do." I tried hard not to grind my teeth every time he insinuated that I wasn't the sharpest knife in the drawer. Being a lawyer required a full head of brains, and I'd been damned good at it, thank you very much. The man was infuriating.

"Those are the flower orders for the next month, so don't forget." He was waiting for me to screw up every time he asked me to do something. I could feel it. And I would die before I gave him that satisfaction.

I smiled and said, "You could email this to her. It would be so much faster and a lot easier."

He grunted, which told me he was not happy. I started noticing this little tell about him from the first day I met him at the Parks' weekly family dinner. Everyone at the table had been beyond surprised by his arrival. Me included. Especially when he said I was the reason his retirement had been cut short and he'd been forced to return to the Park. Like the Park was some sort of hell. Like he didn't miss being the boss here every minute of every day. And the worst thing, like it was my fault that I'd found that dead man on the premises.

The murder at the hotel had been all over the local news, and even down in Florida where Samuel usually lived, he'd heard about it. I suspected he had more than one little spy in town, and for the squealer, my money was on none other than Casey Cushing.

My name had come up several times in the news stories and not necessarily in a most flattering way. I still didn't understand why the local reporter, Tanya Walsh, insinuated that it was my fault the case was bungled early on. I wasn't the law, after all. I was just the concierge at the hotel. Or at least, I was trying to be.

Samuel snapped, "I don't like using the internet. You never know who's reading your personal correspondence."

I refrained from telling him I was certain no government agency was interested in how many carnations or tulips the Park Hotel ordered every month.

"And what if the email doesn't get there? Then we wouldn't have the right flowers in the lobby or in the suites. That would be unacceptable. This way, if the orders get screwed up, I know exactly who to blame." He gave me one of his famous grandfatherly grins. They worked on his grandchildren and other members of staff, but not on me. I saw right through him. He was as mean as a snake.

"I'll drop this off with June, no problem," I finally relented with a big old toothy grin of my own. Besides, I had Miss Charlotte's letter to mail, anyway.

"That's a good girl." He patted my shoulder like I was a golden retriever or something. "Oh, and since you're going, grab all the mail from the office and take it to the post office as well. It's barely a block past June's place." He then strode away in the opposite direction. He may have had a little extra pep in his step, too. I resisted the urge to stick my tongue out at his retreating back.

CHAPTER THREE

SINCE I WAS NOW on hotel business and had a plethora of letters and parcels to take to the post office, I decided to pilfer one of the golf carts from the clubhouse—they frowned upon that, but I was feeling wild and crazy, I guess—and drive it down the hill to the village.

Daisy's Pet Hotel was situated right at the bottom of the hill and would've been as far as I needed to go, so I had to adjust my route. It would take me a bit longer to get back to the kennels, but it would all be worth it in the end when I could sit with Scout and Jem and pet their furry little heads. They always made me feel better, calmer, more relaxed. And relaxing wasn't something I'd done in more days than I cared to count.

Partly, I was uneasy about this business of moving to Hong Kong. On the one hand, my parents were right. There was nothing holding me here now. I'd been suspended from my job at the law firm, and I wasn't really wanted or needed here at the Park. Well, not everyone here felt that way. But Samuel certainly did, and he made no secret of it. But I wasn't married, no kids, no home really. There was nothing at all tying me down.

Which wasn't the issue. When my parents moved to Hong Kong, they'd left me behind. At first, I'd been defiant about it, of course. What fifteen-year-old wouldn't be? There we were, living happily in the suburbs in a nice house with nice schools and nice friends. Then one day, just like that, Dad comes home and says we're moving to Hong Kong. *Hong Kong*! Seriously? Leave my school, my friends, my boyfriend, everything I knew and loved in the word to move to *Hong Kong*? After days and weeks of arguments, pleading, tears, and a lot of foot stomping, they'd moved without me. Left me and Miss Charlotte behind. On our own. After a few months of shocked disbelief, we'd been just fine, thank you very much.

I'd graduated from high school, moved on to college, met Ginny, and her family became mine. After that, law school and a great job in California. Everything was going along well. Really well. I'd thought. Until my boss stole millions from our clients, and I got suspended.

But none of what had happened ever made me want to move to *Hong Kong*. Not now. Not ever. My parents would simply need to get used to it.

I drove down the road from the hotel onto Main Street, which ran along the water, both sides of the street crammed with quaint shops selling boutique items and touristy treasures. Beyond them lay the fishing docks and ferry piers. I turned onto Rose Lane just past Daisy's kennels and went up Market Street.

I passed the hospital, a couple of historic houses built in the 1800s, the sheriff's office—I resisted childishly sticking my tongue out in that general direction—town hall, and the court offices, and then parked in front of the post office, which was an old stone building that had seen better days.

I took all the mail and parcels inside to the man who worked the counter. Jerry was his name. As we went through everything, he chatted nonstop about the weather and the upcoming Flower Festival. He loved all the festivities, especially the pie-eating contest, which he had been preparing for all winter and spring by eating a ton of pies. The prize this year was the same as every year. Two hundred dollars and a year's supply of pie from Patty's Homestyle Pies and Cakes.

After we were done sorting through everything and the parcels were signed for, I posted my letter to Miss Charlotte in Texas, then returned to the cart. I turned around to go back to June's Blooms, which just happened to be across the street from town hall and the sheriff's office. I really hoped I didn't run into Sheriff Jackson today. I'd only seen him once since the wrap-up of the murder, and even then, I barely got a "hello, how do you do?" out of him.

Maybe because I had tried to tell him how to do his job during the investigation. It was quite possible that I had been a bit too bossy and superior about it all at the time. But I just didn't understand why he was reluctant to take advantage of my expertise, especially after I informed him that I had studied criminal law and knew something about crime scenes and such.

In the end, I guess I showed him what my brain can do. Could be that worried him most of all—me getting under his feet all the time. He certainly seemed to be avoiding me. Which was fine by me. Samuel kept me on my toes enough as it was. I didn't need Sheriff Jackson added to the tension.

I went inside the flower shop as the tiny tinkling bell atop the door announced my arrival. The two little parakeets in the cage near the door chimed in.

"Customer!" the blue one squawked.

June came out of the back room, her cat-eye glasses perched on top of her head. The frames were pink and nearly disappeared among the red strands of her hair.

"Andi. How nice to see you." She beamed at me, and it made me smile in return. Every time I'd seen her, she was glowing with joy and light.

"Hi, June." I set the envelope down on the counter. "I'm here to drop off the flower orders for next month."

She picked up the envelope and opened it, sliding the papers out. "I don't know how many times I've told Mr. Park to just email the orders. Easier for me to fill them and to keep track of everything that way. Gotta be easier for the Park, too."

"Yeah, well, I tried telling him that…"

She chuckled. "He is set in his ways."

"That he is."

"Did you come down just to deliver this?"

I shook my head. "I'm headed to check up on my cats over at Daisy's."

"Oh, could you do me a favor since you're going?"

"Sure."

She ducked into the back and returned with a bag full of dandelions. "For Daisy's guinea pigs. A special treat."

I grabbed the large bag and grinned. "Happy to do it. See you later, June."

I opened the door and walked out onto the street. The sun was low in the sky, and it nearly blinded me. Putting my hand up to block the glare, I nearly ran right into Sheriff Jackson. He stumbled backward to avoid my elbows, which were raised to carry the big bag of weeds. He succeeded, but his coffee wasn't as lucky. It ended up all over his form-fitting jeans.

My stomach dropped, and I pressed my lips together, grimacing.

"I'm so sorry, Sheriff."

He sighed, as he often did around me, and shook his head. "No, it was my fault. I saw the hotel golf cart out front and should've anticipated running into you at some point."

The way he said it sounded like I was some kind of natural disaster. Like the golf cart was an early warning signal for Hurricane Andi.

"Um, okay, not sure what that means, but…"

"It means I accept your apology. Okay? Simple. Nothing sinister."

"Fine." I nodded to him, then dropped my bag of dandelions onto the seat of the cart and jumped behind the wheel.

He took off his hat, ran a hand through his hair, and shook his head at me again. I'd always thought he'd look more at home on a Texas ranch than on an island in the middle of Lake Michigan. He had a certain cowboy-like swagger about him. Then he plunked his hat on and strode toward the coffee shop to get himself another coffee.

I did a U-turn in the middle of the street, not caring if the sheriff was watching, and raced down Market Street to Daisy's kennels. I probably looked like a total idiot trying to peel out in my little cart and flaunt the law in front of the sheriff. I imagined him having a little chuckle at my expense.

I parked in front of Daisy's place and went inside, instantly greeted by the business's mascot, a ginormous dog with a boxy head named Rufus. He was a Great Dane/pit bull mix, and he was the sweetest dog I'd ever come across. I scratched him behind his ears and cooed to him. I loved dogs, almost as much as I loved cats, and Rufus brought out the canine maternal instinct in me.

"Who's a good boy?"

He gave a soft *woof* in answer to my question.

Daisy came out from the back kennels. The symphony of canine and feline greetings followed in her wake.

"Hi, Daisy. I came to see my babies." I put the sack of dandelions on the counter. "June sends her regards."

With eager eyes and hands, Daisy grabbed the bag of weeds. "Oh, Petunia and Lance are going to be fine-dining for weeks on this."

I followed her into the back, to where the official deluxe rooms of the pet hotel were. No actual kennel for my loves, for sure. Scout and Jem had a nice suite, with a big scratching post, several shelves on the walls to lounge on, an old chair they could scratch the stuffing out of, and a series of tunnels and bridges up high along the ceiling. It was like the presidential palace for cats.

I went inside and was instantly greeted with meows. I sat on the floor and fed them special treats and petted them until my hands were sore. We'd never spent much time away from each other, and I missed them like crazy. But I knew they were being very well cared for. Truth was, I worried that they'd come to love Daisy more than they loved me.

I picked up Scout and whispered in her ear, "It won't be long, I promise. Another couple of months, and we'll be going back home. I'll be a lawyer again, and you'll be happy Cali kitties again."

After another half hour, I kissed them both goodbye and wandered out front, where Daisy was busy scowling over some papers.

"Thanks, Daisy," I said. "They seem really happy."

She looked up and smiled. "Oh, they're great cats. They totally miss you, though—don't fret about that. Pets always miss their owners." Then she went back to scowling at the paper on her desk. The scowl was so odd on her usually sunny face.

"What's that? Looks like it's giving you some problems."

"Lease agreement. I think my landlord is totally screwing me, but I can't quite figure out how."

"Want me to take a look? I did a lot of contract law coming up at the law firm I worked for back in California."

She puffed out her cheeks. "Oh, would you? You're an angel." She rolled up the contract and handed it to me. "Oh, and while you're being an angel, do you think you could help me take some birdseed to a client of mine? It's a pain carrying it up on my bike, and seeing as you got the cart and all..." She pointed out the window and gave me a very toothy smile.

Who could resist that?

"Sure, why not? I'm on a favor roll right now."

"Awesome!"

Mrs. Walker, Daisy's client, was eighty years old and didn't get around that well. So, Daisy brought big bags of seed to Mrs. Walker's house and fed the birds for her. I didn't mind helping. Daisy was one of those people you instinctively wanted to help if you had any kind of heart.

I parked the cart in front of the two-story red-brick house. It looked like it was built in the 1920s with the front veranda and a tiny little patio off the second-floor bedroom. We went around the back through the kitchen, which Daisy told me was always unlocked. Which wasn't odd at all. Not many people locked their doors in the village.

We walked in, and I noticed there were some groceries in brown paper bags on the kitchen counter. I peered inside to make sure there wasn't anything thawing inside—maybe Mrs. Walker had forgotten about them.

"She gets the groceries delivered to her once a week as well. Looks like the boy forgot to put them away." She started to take out what was inside the bags. "I'll just do this quickly. Why don't you go into the living room and feed the two birds in the cage there." She handed me some seed.

When I gave her a look, she laughed. "It's easy. Just put it into the little metal bowl hanging from the middle of the cage. Lucy and Desi won't bite. There're good little dudes."

Taking the seed, I walked out of the kitchen and into the small living room. The birdcage was near the front window. The two tiny birds inside chirped happily as I neared. I reached inside to fill the bowl, and one of them nipped at my finger.

"Ouch." I scowled at it. "That hurt." I inspected my finger, saw a small bead of blood. "Wow, my day off isn't going so well, is it?"

And that's when I spied the staircase that led to the second level near the front door. Sunlight streamed in through the stained-glass windows in the sidelights, cascading red and yellow light onto the floor.

Illuminating Mrs. Walker's twisted body at the bottom of the stairs.

Chapter Four

WHY ME? THAT WAS the question that kept scrolling through my mind as I rubbed a hand up and down Daisy's back, trying to calm her as we waited for an ambulance and the sheriff to arrive. Two bodies in two months. Must have been some kind of record for a concierge who didn't work directly in law enforcement. It wasn't really a record I wanted.

Once I'd seen Mrs. Walker's body, I had checked for a pulse—my hands shaking the whole time, even though I was going for an aura of calm—and found none. Then I went back into the kitchen to tell Daisy. At first she just blinked at me, likely trying to compute what I'd just told her, and then she walked into the living room to see for herself.

I'd seen people in shock before, and that was exactly what she was experiencing. After she saw the body, her eyes went wide and her mouth went slack, so I escorted her back to the kitchen, sat her down, and proceeded to make the necessary calls. I told both the 9-1-1 operator and Deputy Shawn to come through the back door, since Mrs. Walker was sort of blocking the front door.

"Are you sure she's dead?" Daisy asked me for the third time.

"Yes. I'm sorry."

Daisy wiped at her mouth and then took another sip of the water I'd retrieved for her. "I can't believe it. I mean, she's in her eighties...*was* in her eighties," she corrected, "so I knew eventually she'd pass on, but falling down the stairs? That's a crappy way to die."

I nodded in agreement. It was a horrible way to go.

While we waited, I examined the kitchen, taking mental notes of different things. The bright, tiny room was neat and tidy besides the grocery bag, which was now empty because Daisy had put away the contents.

I wondered if Mrs. Walker had someone come in to clean. She must have. I couldn't picture her puttering around, scrubbing the counters and sink. The room almost looked unused. I took in the flowered wallpaper and slightly discolored linoleum floor, which seemed so typical of old houses like this. Then my gaze flittered over the square flap in the bottom of the back door.

"Where's the dog?" I asked.

"What?"

"There's a doggy door. Where's her dog?"

Daisy sagged lower in her seat. "So sad. Little Lulu went missing about a week ago."

"That's awful. What kind of dog?"

"Pekinese. A cute thing, but so yappy. Lulu barked constantly."

Before I could ask anything more, the back door into the kitchen opened and Sheriff Jackson walked in, followed by the tall, pixie-haired doctor from the hospital, Dr. Neumann. The last time I'd seen her was over the outstretched legs of a screaming young woman having a baby.

I looked the sheriff over and noticed he'd changed his pants from our earlier caffeine collision. I wondered if he had a whole slew of jeans folded away somewhere in his office. I also wondered if he ever wore anything else.

"This is Dr. Neumann. This is Andi Steele."

The doctor nodded sharply.

"We've met," I said.

Sheriff Jackson gave me a look, but I said nothing more.

"Right." He nodded. "Where's Mrs. Walker?"

I led them through the living room to the front foyer where the body was. This time, I noticed her cane lying on the step above her. I hadn't noticed it before. It's amazing the little things you focus on in times of tragedy. Like the repetitive ticking of the cuckoo clock on the foyer wall, the continual chirping of the birds in the cage nearby, or the way the yellow light through the front door sidelight played across Mrs. Walker's pale, wrinkled hand. I shuddered, wanting to wrap myself in my arms.

Sheriff Jackson looked at me curiously. I shook myself out of my brain fog and moved away from the body so the doctor could do her thing. Dr. Neumann immediately crouched next to Mrs. Walker and checked her non-existent vitals, then started to look over the body under the sheriff's watchful eye. I hung back and put my attention on the framed pictures on the walls.

Most were of painted flowers and landscapes. Prints, not originals. There were only three actual photos. One was, I assumed, a younger Mrs. Walker, in her sixties maybe, a portrait. She sat in a high-backed chair, the one I'd spotted in the living room, wearing a floral blouse and dour black skirt. Her hair was nicely coiffed, and a set of pearls rested at her throat. She wasn't smiling. She looked like a very sad woman.

The other photo was of her, much younger, and two other people, a man and a woman. They all looked similar, so possibly her siblings or cousins. Again, she had no smile but was wearing the pearl necklace. The others were grinning like fools. I wondered whether she had contact with them anymore.

The sheriff came up to my side, took out his little notebook, and gave me that look of frustration that he always seemed to display any time I was around.

"You know the drill," he said with pen poised over paper.

I proceeded to tell him the time we arrived at the house (2:25 p.m.), that the back door was open (Daisy told me it was always unlocked), that there was a bag of groceries on the counter when we came in, and that I found the body accidentally while feeding the birds in the living room.

"Did you know the deceased?"

"No. I was just here doing a favor for Daisy."

"And you know Daisy…how?"

"My two cats are temporarily boarded at her pet hotel."

He closed his notebook. "Okay. You can go."

"I'd rather just wait until Daisy can leave. I'll drive her back to her place."

He was about to say something when the doctor stood and came over. "She definitely fell and broke her neck."

"Time of death?" the sheriff asked.

"It's always a guess, as you know. But rigor's not set, so I'd say no more than two hours ago."

"Okay, thanks, Doc."

She nodded to me again and left the house through the back door.

Sheriff Jackson went over to Daisy to take her statement. "Andi told me most of it, but I just want to ask you a few follow-ups."

"Sure."

"How often do you visit Mrs. Walker?" he asked.

"I come every Monday with seed for the birds, and I feed them for her. She can't get around too good. Couldn't," Daisy corrected and shook her head. I could see the tears forming in her eyes, and I grabbed her hand. She gave me a pitiful smile. "She used a cane to help her walk."

"You have a key to the house?"

Daisy nodded. "But only to be used for emergencies. The back door is usually open this time of day."

"Andi mentioned there was a bag of groceries on the counter when you arrived."

"Yes. I put them away for her, and then Andi called out to me about...you know, finding Mrs. Walker."

"Does Mrs. Walker do her own grocery shopping? I didn't see a car in front of the house, so I just wondered, since she can't get around well."

Daisy shrugged. "I'm pretty sure she gets home delivery."

"She doesn't have relatives who help her out?" he asked.

"The only relatives she has on the island, as far as I know, are Peter and Colleen Walker. I think Peter is her great-nephew. She didn't talk very highly of him, though. Called him an ingrate on more than one occasion." She shook her head and smiled wistfully. "She didn't suffer fools easily. She was a grumpy old lady, but I dug her, you know? Although I don't think many did."

He nodded, then closed his notebook. "Thanks. That's all I need. You two can get on home now."

"Thanks, Sheriff." Daisy got to her feet and then frowned. "What will happen to her birds?"

"That will be up to her next of kin. Probably this Peter Walker."

"Could you let him know that I will gladly take them if he doesn't want them?"

"I'll let him know." He tipped his hat to us and then wandered back toward the body.

I clenched my hands, knowing that I had no business following him. I had done my duty as a witness, and now my responsibility was to get Daisy back to work.

Daisy opened the back door, looking at me over her shoulder expectedly.

My index finger came up. "Just give me one second."

I fast-walked over to where the sheriff stood looking down at the body, and then he looked up at the staircase. He turned and flashed a scowl at me when I stepped up beside him. "Shouldn't you be going home?"

"This *was* an accident, right?"

He sighed. "Andi, please take Daisy back to the kennels, then drive that cart back to the hotel, pour a glass of wine, and have a hot bath, or whatever it is you do to relax."

"That's not really an answer."

His brow furrowed deeper as he looked at me. For one fleeting moment, I wanted to reach up and smooth away those lines with the pad of my thumb. He always looked so weary, like he carried so much more than the weight of this town on his shoulders. "You're testing my patience...again."

The sensation vanished like a puff of gray smoke.

I lifted a lip in a half grimace. "I'm going. And I do Sudoku to relax, for your information."

"Figures," I heard him mumble before I was out of earshot.

I joined Daisy at the back door. "What was that about?" she asked.

"Nothing. I thought I left my purse over there."

Her one eyebrow came up as she stared directly at the red leather pouch sitting at my hip, the strap across my chest. The one that had been there the entire time, where it always was. I shooed her out the door.

As we crossed the yard toward the golf cart parked on the street, the front door of the neighboring house opened, and an elderly man in a plaid shirt, denim jeans, and suspenders shuffled out. A blue baseball hat settled on his sparsely haired head.

"What's going on?" he asked gruffly.

Daisy ignored him, so I did, too. I didn't know the man, and I really didn't want to be spreading rumors.

He leaned over the railing of his porch and barked, "Did something happen to Ida?"

"I'm sure the sheriff will come talk to you about it, Mr. Rainer," Daisy said.

He huffed and mumbled, "That woman's always causing trouble." He then shuffled back into his house and slammed the door shut.

I glanced at Daisy. "What was that all about? He doesn't seem very friendly."

"He's not. He's actually quite nasty." She shook her head. "I've been present a couple of times when he's shouted at Mrs. Walker. He even called her the B word once. I'd been shocked, but it didn't faze Mrs. Walker. She called him worse in return."

"What was he so angry about?"

"Everything. He complained about Mrs. Walker's yard being too weedy, about the fence being too low, about the birds squawking at all hours of the day and night."

"Yikes."

"But most of the time, it was about little Lulu. He was always complaining about the dog. Saying how much noise she made, about how useless she was. Mrs. Walker said he hated that dog. I think he hates all animals, to be honest."

"You don't think he had anything to do with Lulu's disappearance, do you?" I shuddered at the mere thought of something like that happening. But the truth was people could do horrible things when motivated by frustration or rage or a chance for revenge. I'd seen those emotions put into action firsthand recently when I'd discovered the dead body at the hotel.

Daisy frowned. "I'd be lying if I said the thought hadn't crossed my mind a time or two."

We jumped into the cart, and I started it up. As we pulled away from the curb, I glanced at Mr. Rainer's house. I could see his face peering out from behind the curtains in the front window, and he didn't look too happy.

CHAPTER FIVE

AFTER I DROPPED DAISY off at the kennels, I drove back up to
the Park. I returned the cart to its designated spot—thankfully,
no one called me out for taking it off premises—and then entered
the lobby of the hotel. The second I was through the doors,
Ginny pounced on me.

"I heard about old Mrs. Walker."

I gaped at her. "How did you hear so fast?"

"Let's see…Mrs. Duka lives across the street, and she saw
the doc and the sheriff pull up. So, she called her daughter Anna,
who does hair at the salon on Main. Bethany Atkins was getting
her brows waxed. Bethany is Vicki's mother. That's Vicki who
works at the tea house. So, we all pretty much knew shortly after
that."

The words tumbled out of her without a breath between
them. Fascinating. She should have taken up long-distance
swimming with those lungs.

I shook my head. The speed at which information and gossip traveled around this island was amazing. Ten times better than the internet and didn't cost a cent.

She put her hand on my arm. "Are you okay?"

"I'm fine."

She gave me a look.

"I know. How can a girl be so lucky?" I chuckled.

"You know what you need?"

"No." I was afraid of what she was going to suggest. The last time she asked that question, we were in college. We both got drunk, and I ended up plastic-wrapping her bed with her brother Eric's help. The hangover caused me to swear off booze for years.

"A night out. Since you've been on the island, we haven't gone to any of the bars for a few drinks and some good music and fun."

"Not sure I'm up for socializing, Ginny."

"C'mon." She wrapped a hand around my arm. "You can't just work all day and sequester yourself in your suite all night. It's not healthy. You need to be around people. You need to drink, and eat, and laugh, and flirt with some sexy guy who's entirely no good for you."

That made me think of Mayor Daniel Evans. He was a sexy guy, but he was probably entirely *too* good for me. His business card burned a hole in my wallet. I'd been tempted a time or two to call him, like he'd invited me to, but then I thought of a million reasons why it was a bad idea:

1. He was too good looking and single—something had to be wrong with him.

2. He was the mayor of the town on the mainland. Pretty sure that would be seen as disloyal to the islanders.

3. I didn't want to fall in love when I knew I'd be leaving the second I got the cloud off my license.

"I don't know…"

"Oh, c'mon. Please. It *is* your day off, after all." She literally batted her eyelashes at me, while her puffy lips turned down in a pout. Oh, she was good. No wonder she got men of all ages to do whatever she wanted.

"Fine. I'll think about it."

She smiled. "Well, that's definitely the firmest answer I'm going to get out of you. So, I'll take it."

"But now? Now I'm going to go to my suite, grab some food, and sit out on my patio and read." I was determined to do this today, and nothing was going to stop me, not Ginny, not poor dead Mrs. Walker, not anything.

"Okay, I'll text you later about hitting the bar. Swan Song has karaoke tonight." She mimicked holding a microphone and did her best Tina Turner impression.

I laughed. "Absolutely no karaoke."

"All right, not this time," she said, giggling.

"Not ever," I said more firmly.

I hugged her, then before I could set off toward my suite, one of the servers from the restaurant—she was still in her uniform—came out of the restaurant crying. She rubbed at her nose and was saying something into her phone.

"Who's that?" I asked Ginny.

"Colleen Walker."

My eyebrows came up. "Related to Mrs. Walker?"

She nodded. "Yeah, her husband Peter is Mrs. Walker's great-nephew."

"Oh, that's sad for them, I'm sure."

Ginny harrumphed.

"What?"

"It's just that I've never known Colleen to be sad about anything, especially not her great-aunt," Ginny said.

The Walkers seemed to have an interesting family dynamic going on. Well, interesting to me, at least. But then, my own family dynamic was nothing to brag about, either. "Really?" I asked as casually as I could. I wanted to shout, *Tell me more!* But that would have been just plain rude.

"Colleen's never said a nice word about her once. In fact, in the past, she has spewed quite a lot of venom about the old woman."

My eye twitched, and I started chewing my cuticles. Anything to keep me from asking questions.

Ginny narrowed her gaze at me. "Don't even think about it, Andi."

"What?"

"You have that look in your eyes again," she said.

"Don't be silly. I'm just a concerned citizen."

"Right. You're a horrible liar, you know? You've never been any good at it. Good thing you never tried to be a criminal lawyer."

I pouted. "I think I always find out the truth."

"Yeah, but you could never have represented anyone who was guilty. Your face would have given him away every time."

I shrugged. "True." I tracked Colleen with my eyes as she walked across the lobby and outside. I wished I could hear her phone conversation. "Okay, text me later," I said, then wandered off toward the lobby doors.

"Andi, your suite is not that way."

"I just need some air." I didn't wait for her response, because she would only tell me to mind my own business, that there wasn't anything nefarious going on. That Mrs. Walker falling down those stairs was just an accident and nothing sinister.

Colleen stood on the sidewalk along the hotel courtyard, still on her phone. I walked toward her, then stopped and pretended to be digging around in my purse for something. It was a classic eavesdropping move and so much easier for women to get away with—we almost always had a purse full of unnecessary junk. While men…well, all they had were some sad little pockets to dig through. That feat would take a mere couple of minutes, while I could literally be sorting through the things in my bag for a half hour and no one would be suspicious.

Now that she was out of the hotel lobby, Colleen didn't look so tearful. She wiped at her cheeks, almost angrily. "She better have left us the house, Peter. We haven't put up with her crap all these years for no reason."

That's some seriously cold thinking right there.

"I know we'll have to wait until the reading of the will to finalize the deed, but there's nothing saying we can't start moving her stuff out and ours in, is there?"

Yikes. I didn't like the sound of that.

I must've made some kind of disapproving noise in my throat because Colleen whipped around and shot eye daggers at me. I froze, with my arm elbow-deep inside my purse. Quickly, I yanked it out with my phone in my hand. I did the *pretend answer* trick and walked away. Before I turned the corner of the hotel, I glanced over my shoulder. She was still watching me.

Once I was safely out of view, I slid my phone back into my purse and booked it around the long length of the hotel to go back in through one of the side doors. I wasn't sure what I was going to do, but I had to do something, tell someone. I stopped in my tracks and gave my head a shake.

No, I'm not going to do anything, because there isn't anything to do. I was being presumptuous about a fairly innocent phone call from a woman to her husband about the death of their great-aunt. Just because I thought Colleen was horrible and said mean things about Mrs. Walker, didn't mean she'd done anything intentionally malicious.

Mrs. Walker fell down her stairs accidentally. There was no indication anything was amiss.

Although…the sheriff had been studying those stairs intently, and there was the matter of the bag of groceries being left on the counter—when, why, and by whom—and the feuding with the nasty neighbor over her dog. Honestly, pushing a frail old lady down a set of stairs was a plausible way to murder her while making it look like an accident.

Just to satisfy my own curiosity, I would simply borrow the golf cart again and pop down to the village and ask around about Peter and Colleen Walker. The way people liked to talk in this town, I'd know everything I needed to know and then some about the couple in an hour or less. The trip would hardly put a dent in my planned relaxing evening. I'd still have time to sit out on my patio and read my book before the sun dropped or before Ginny made me go out with her to the bar.

My first stop was to the Weiss Strudel House on Main Street. I grabbed two cherry strudels for my next stop and an apple strudel for me. As I walked the two blocks up to the ferry dock, I devoured the pastry. I'd never tasted better and had to admit I'd become a regular patron of the old German couple, Wilhelm and Lena, who owned and operated the place. We were on a first-name basis now. I always got a hardy "Hello, Andi" from both when I walked in.

The next stop was the dock where all the best and most up-to-date information could be had for the price of a couple of cherry strudels. I found JC and Reggie, as usual, at their table playing chess and arguing about something that probably happened twenty years ago and they still didn't agree on.

JC looked up, squinting into the setting sun as I approached. *"Bon soir, ma jolie dame."*

I smiled. Despite JC's advanced age, he was still a charmer. I imagined he was quite the lady killer when he was young. Although from the way I heard it around town, he only had eyes for one lady, and that had been his wife Rose. They'd been married for over fifty years before she passed away from cancer a couple of years ago.

I placed the strudel bag on the table. "I come bearing gifts."

Reggie took his strudel and immediately chowed down, while pastry flakes dropped all over his grizzled chin. "Thanks, Andi."

"You're welcome."

JC narrowed his eyes at me. "And what can we do for you this fine evening?"

I shrugged. "Nothing. Just was in the neighborhood."

"Uh-huh," he said, eyeing me suspiciously. "I heard old lady Walker had herself an accident."

I nodded. "Yeah, it was terrible."

"Let me guess. You found her." Reggie shook his head. "You have some serious bad luck, little lady."

"Yeah, I'm starting to think that." I asked my question carefully. "Did either of you know her?"

JC nodded. "Oh, yup, we knew Ida. She was someone you couldn't ignore."

"She was a cranky old boot," Reggie added.

"You'd know, wouldn't you? You had a thing with her way back when." JC cackled at his own words.

Reggie frowned. "No, I didn't."

"You did too. You took her to the formal back in '52."

"That was Eddie Black that took her, you dumb ass." He flicked his pastry-flecked fingers at him across the table.

"Ah, yup, that's right." JC conceded. "Old Eddie. He died in '09. Liver cancer."

Reggie nodded in agreement as they paused to think about their old friend.

"She have family around?" I asked, trying to get things back on track. My particular track.

JC pursed his lips as he pondered, then he nodded. "Yup, Peter, I think. Her great-nephew. She never married or had kids of her own. Poor Peter."

"Yeah, I heard that she wasn't very nice to him."

JC shrugged. "Could be. But I meant Poor Peter as in Poor Peter—that's what people call him. He hasn't ever got any money. He comes into the Vic sometimes, and everyone says, 'Oh hey, there's Poor Peter.'"

"Yeah, then we all hide our wallets." Reggie guffawed.

JC laughed, too, then he said, "Guess we won't be calling him that anymore, I reckon."

"Why's that?"

"Well, he'd be getting all her money, I reckon. From what I heard around town, she had quite a bit sacked away. She didn't have anything to spend it on. Her house was free and clear for twenty years now, I'd guess."

"From her teacher pension?" Reggie frowned. "Not likely."

"Nah, I guess old Ida was smart with the numbers. She made some investments years ago, and now they're worth something."

"What kind of investments?" Reggie asked before I could.

"In the computer market, I heard. You know, that Gates fella. Whatever company he started."

I gaped at him. "You mean Microsoft? She invested in Microsoft?"

JC shrugged. "Could be. Could be. Guess we'll know soon enough when Poor Peter comes to the pub and buys us all a drink." He smacked his hand on his knee and laughed so hard he started to cough.

I chatted a bit longer before I bid them a good evening and headed back to the hotel. I had a lot to digest and put together about what Reggie and JC had told me. If I had it right, Peter and his wife Colleen had one hell of a motive to send their poor great-aunt Ida to an early grave.

Chapter Six

I NEVER MADE IT to the hotel—at least not then. Since I was already out and about, I decided to drive the golf cart to the D&W Fresh Market over on Blossom Lane. I needed some fresh fruit, bagels, and eggs for my suite. It just happened to be a lucky coincidence that I'd noticed the name of that grocery store on the paper bag of groceries that had been on Mrs. Walker's kitchen counter. Whoever delivered her groceries may have seen something. Not that there was necessarily anything to see at the time. But that would be good to know, too. Might help establish time of death.

I walked in, grabbed a hand basket, and collected my produce. At the till, I chatted up the young female clerk whose name tag read *Hannah*. "You guys do home delivery, right?"

She nodded. "We sure do."

"Is it always the same delivery people?"

Hannah didn't look at me as she weighed and rung up my bag of purple table grapes. "We got two guys who do all the deliveries. Carter and Todd."

"Who was working today?"

She finally glanced up as she tallied my final total. I noticed a dark patch on her cheek. Looked like it might be a bruise covered up with hurried makeup. There was also a bruise peeking out from her sleeve on her uniform. Poor girl. I really hoped that her bruises were not a domestic issue. I had a zero tolerance policy for men who hit women.

She frowned. "It was Todd doing deliveries today. Did you have a problem with your delivery, ma'am? I can call the manager for you."

I was about to tell her *yes, I'd love to talk to the manager*, when I spotted Sheriff Jackson entering the store. He didn't look like he was there to shop. Instead of going down the aisles into the store, he headed straight for the customer service desk, which was just one cash register over from where I was.

I didn't want him to see me because he'd get cranky about why I was there. And he'd be right. I wasn't just picking up some snacks; I was making inquiries. Inquires I had no real business making. *Hey, a girl can go to the grocery store any damn time she wants to. I have nothing to hide.*

But I decided to hide, anyway.

"You know what? I have a few more things I need to get." I lifted my purse up to cover my face. "Do you think you could just put this all to the side for me?"

The clerk gaped at me, at my ten items, at the people in line behind me, then at me again.

"I know it's an inconvenience," I said. "I'm really sorry." I didn't wait for her response but turned around and walked quickly down the aisle. The other two people in line shook their heads.

One older lady *tsk*ed under her breath. "Tourists," I heard her say.

I hightailed it down the frozen-food aisle, as far away from the customer service desk as I could get. I ended up near the meat counter and pretended to be inspecting the fish cutlets.

In my periphery, I spotted a young man in a green D&W shirt and black pants walking in my direction. Hands jammed into his pockets, he was licking his lips, and his gaze, which was aimed at the ground, flitted back and forth. I'd seen *guilty of something syndrome* before, and this guy had it in spades. As he passed me, I read the back of his shirt: D&W Delivers.

He pushed through the "employees only" door and disappeared. I was just about to follow when a big guy in a bloody white apron popped up behind the counter, startling me.

"What can I get you?" he asked.

"Oh, I'm just looking right now."

"How about a nice piece of whitefish? Freshly caught." He picked up a thick fillet and presented it to me like he was showing off a Rolex to a wealthy businessman.

"No, I don't think—"

"Andi?"

I turned to see Sheriff Jackson approaching me, and I said to the butcher, "Oh, yes, that's perfect. Thank you."

The butcher frowned, looking confused for a moment about my abrupt change of mind, but he quickly shook it off and went to wrap up my fish in brown paper.

"Just getting some fish," I said to the sheriff as he regarded me with that suspicious crinkle in his forehead.

"Something you suddenly needed when you spotted me coming into the store?"

I gave him a look. "I don't know what you mean."

"Uh-huh. And you're not shopping here because you want to ask questions about the grocery delivery to Mrs. Walker?"

"No. Of course I'm not." I made a face, feigning confusion. "I'm human. I eat food. Grocery stores have food. See the chain of logic there?"

His one eyebrow came up, letting me know he didn't believe a word of what I was saying.

I leaned closer to him. "Is that why you're here? Hmm? Not sure her fall was an accident?"

"I'm here to complete my report. Which includes following up on everything."

"Right." I nodded.

The butcher slapped my wrapped fish onto the counter. "There you go, miss." He smiled at me then nodded to the sheriff. "What can I get you, Sheriff?"

"Nothing. Thanks, Bud." He looked pointedly at me again. "Enjoy your fish. Back at the hotel."

I tucked it under my arm. "I will. Thank you." I started back toward the checkout line, Sheriff Jackson watching me the whole time. It was like he didn't trust me to actually leave the store. Smart man.

When I reached the register, there was another clerk there ringing up purchases. All the stuff that I'd grabbed earlier had been shoved into a basket on the floor. I picked it up, got back in line, and slapped my fish down on the conveyor. I guess I was making myself whitefish tonight for dinner, which was a conundrum as I hadn't a clue how to cook whitefish.

The clerk must have been a mind reader, or I was a poor actress like Ginny had implied, because the women looked at my perplexed expression and said, "A little oil, garlic, lemon juice, bake for twelve minutes, and it will be perfect."

I gave her a sheepish grin. "Thank you."

As I packed my grocery bags into the golf cart, something in the parking lot caught my eye. It was that boy I'd seen inside when I was not buying and then was buying fish. He was huddled in the corner near the store, smoking and talking on the phone. He appeared to be severely agitated, hurriedly pacing back and forth in the tiny area like a caged animal.

I was about to creep a little closer in my golf cart so I could hear the conversation when I saw the sheriff walk out of the store and head toward him. Not wanting to tempt fate or tempt Sheriff Jackson into giving me more than just a subtle warning to stay away, I started the golf cart and got the hell out of Dodge.

Chapter Seven

AS I WAITED AT the stop sign to turn onto Ivy Street to head back to Market, then up the hill to the hotel, an old man on a big tricycle turned in front of me. I looked over as he passed and saw that it was Mr. Rainer. But the most surprising part of that was he had a big bag of dog food in the basket behind him. As far as I knew, or that Daisy had told me, Mr. Rainer didn't have a dog and had hated Mrs. Walker's little Pekinese.

The little voice in my head told me to just return to the hotel. None of this was my business.

"Oh shut it," I said, and did a U-turn.

I tried to keep a good distance between us, as it was extremely difficult to stay inconspicuous in a golf cart with the words *The Park Hotel* printed in gold and red letters on the side. It proved easier, though, since I knew exactly where Mr. Rainer was headed.

I parked on the street a block down from the Rainer and Walker houses. I wasn't quite sure what my play would be here, but I had to find out what was going on with Mr. Rainer. As subtly as I could, I strolled down the sidewalk as if I were merely on a pleasant walk through the neighborhood.

When I reached the Rainer house, I checked all the windows to make sure he wasn't looking out and then jogged up alongside the house. Pressing my back along the wall, I made my way toward the back yard. I peered around the corner and saw it was blocked off by a blockade fence. Crouching, I peered through a small gap in the wooden slats.

The yard was cluttered with empty clay flower pots, old white plastic lawn chairs, and a broken table that leaned heavily to the right. The grass was a bit overgrown, and there were a few dandelions along the fence, but there was no evidence of any canine in sight. No plastic water dishes or abandoned leashes or rope. No bouncy rubber balls or rawhide chew toys lying forgotten in the weeds. Nothing to suggest a dog lived there.

Turning around, I slid back to the front of the house. I crept up onto the porch, freezing still on one of the steps when it made a loud creaking noise. When the door didn't open and a cranky old man didn't emerge, I continued until I was pressed up against the wall near the big front window. The curtains were drawn tight, but they were a white filmy material, and if I pressed my face to the glass, I could sort of see inside.

Through the haze, I could make out the living room. It was sparsely decorated with a sofa that had its heyday in the 1970s, an easy chair that looked worn and frayed from use, an old wooden table covered with magazines, empty plates, and glasses. I wondered when was the last time a woman had set foot in Mr. Rainer's house. Looked like maybe it had been a decade, if ever.

I didn't see him anywhere, not at first. But then movement from the left caught my attention, and Mr. Rainer came into the room. He was holding something. Squinting to get a clearer view, I noticed that the something in his arms squirmed around. He sat on the sofa and placed that something on the cushion beside him. It jumped onto his lap and wagged its little furry tail.

A small dog.

I pulled away from the window and knocked on Mr. Rainer's door. At first, I didn't think he was going to answer—maybe he had seen me on his porch and was purposely ignoring my knock. I heard a grunt and a quick curse, then the door swung open, and Mr. Rainer's deeply lined faced scowled out at me.

"What do you want?"

"I don't know if you re—"

"You're the girl from earlier. The one with that nosy animal girl."

"Yes. The reason I'm bothering you, Mr. Rainer, is that I wanted to ask you about Mrs. Walker's dog."

"What about it?"

"I was wondering if you knew where it might have gone. From what I understand, Mrs. Walker had reported her dog missing."

His hand was on the door, and it was starting to swing shut. "I don't know what you're talking about."

"You do remember her dog, Lulu? Little Pekinese?"

"Yeah, stupid dog. Always barking. Ida could never take care of that thing."

"So, you don't know what happened to it?"

"No. Now go away."

I put my foot out before he could slam the door shut. Thankfully, he saw it and didn't smash it like I thought he might. "Are you sure you don't know where Lulu is?"

"I already told you—"

"So, then, who's that adorable little Pekinese standing behind you?"

He swirled around to see Lulu right behind him, tongue out, tail happily wagging. She gave a little *woof* as if to say, "Hello."

"Hello, Lulu," I said.

CHAPTER EIGHT

THE DOOR WAS SWIFTLY slammed shut in my face. The motion of it actually reverberated over my skin. Luckily, I had the presence of mind to yank my foot back before it got crushed.

I knocked on the door again. "Mr. Rainer."

But he wasn't going to answer it. Did I blame him? Not really.

I stepped off the porch and walked back to the cart. After rummaging in my purse, I pulled out my phone and called the sheriff. This was definitely information he needed to have. Even if Mr. Rainer had nothing to do with Mrs. Walker's death, he had stolen her dog!

He answered on the second ring. "This is Sheriff Jackson."

"Sheriff, it's Andi Steele."

His trademark sigh came through. "I hope you're calling to tell me how good the fish you bought is tasting right now."

"Of course not. I just saw you, like, half an hour ago. How could I have possibly gone back to the hotel and cooked the fish already?"

"I think you're missing my point."

"Oh no, I got it."

"What can I do for you, then?"

"I know what happened to Mrs. Walker's dog."

"Okay?"

"She reported it missing a week ago." Out of habit, I cocked my hip and put my hand on my waist. I knew he couldn't possibly see my annoyance, but I was sure he could hear it in my voice. I know I could.

"Not news, Andi. I'm the one she called to report it."

"Well, her next-door neighbor, Mr. Rainer, stole Lulu."

There was silence for a moment, then a groan before he asked, "How do you know?"

"Um, because I saw the dog in his house?"

Another sigh, this one a lot longer and angrier. "You haven't been harassing the man, have you?"

"Of course not. I knocked on his door as a concerned citizen, and lo and behold, after he'd told me a flat-out lie about how horrid the dog was, I saw the cute little ball of fur in his living room." There was more silence, and I thought for a second that he'd disconnected the call. "Dog theft in the state of Michigan must be at least a misdemeanor. Regardless of the circumstances, he should be charged, and the dog should be given to Mrs. Walker's next of kin until her will is read, in which case she may have left instructions about the custody of Lulu."

"Are you really attempting to quote the law to me?"

"Yes."

He disconnected. I squeezed my phone in my hand, wishing desperately for an old-school landline, so I could slam the phone down in its cradle. *Damn you, stupid expensive smartphone!* "Argh! What an ass!"

"Are you okay, dear?"

Nearly jumping a foot in the air, I whirled around to see two tiny white-haired ladies, one in a shocking-blue cardigan, and the other with huge black sunglasses that swallowed her face. They were on the sidewalk, smiling at me. I hadn't even heard them approach. They were stealthy octogenarian lady ninjas with walkers.

"I'm fine. Thanks."

"Is it a man?" the one in the blue cardigan asked.

The other one with the sunglasses nodded. "That flushed look you have tells us it's a man."

I shook my head. Well, technically, I *was* angry about a man, but not in the way they probably meant. "It's not a man. It's just the sheriff."

Both Blue and Sunglasses nodded in unison and said, "Ah."

I laughed. "Oh, no, it's not like that."

Sunglasses patted my arm. "It never is, dear. Not at first, anyway."

"Terrible about Ida," Blue said, happily changing the subject.

"Did you know her well?" I asked.

Sunglasses nodded. "Oh yes, we live just across the street."

It was then I realized they were sisters. Maybe even twins. They were the same height, same body structure, and same head full of curly white hair.

"Did you know about Lulu?" I asked.

Blue nodded. "I know she was horrid to that poor animal."

Whoa. Hadn't expected that. "Really?" I frowned. "How so?"

"Oh, she would yell at it," Sunglasses said, "and one time, I saw her kick it."

"She wasn't a very good person," Blue added with a knowing nod to Sunglasses.

"Nope, she sure wasn't."

"Did she fight with all the neighbors?" I asked.

"Oh yeah. I don't think anyone really liked her," Blue said. "Still a shame what happened to her."

Sunglasses nodded. "Such a shame."

"How about Mr. Rainer? Did he fight with her a lot?"

"Oh yeah. They had frequent battles." Blue lowered herself onto the little seat on her candy-apple blue walker. I swore I could hear her bones creak as she did.

"Always arguing about Lulu," Sunglasses said. "I don't think he liked how she treated that dog. Would never come out and say it, though, but it was in his eyes."

"Yeah, out of everyone on the block," Blue said, "Clark disliked Ida the most. She knew it, too. She said to me once, 'I swear that man's going to kill me one day.'"

Before I could respond to that, the sheriff pulled up in his jeep. He parked behind the cart, got out, and walked over. Well, swaggered, actually. I wanted to ask him what was up his butt, but I had a feeling the answer might be…me.

Blue elbowed me in the side surprisingly hard and wriggled her eyebrows comically.

"Ow." I rubbed at my potentially bruised rib.

"Ladies." He tipped his hat to the elderly women, who were both blushing.

"Hello, Sheriff," Sunglasses said.

His gaze landed on me. "Andi."

"I didn't think you'd show up."

"I take all reported crimes seriously," he said, "I also called Daisy to come get the dog. She can take care of it until matters get settled with the next of kin." He tipped his hat again, then walked up to Mr. Rainer's door and knocked.

Both Blue and Sunglasses watched him walk away with twin appreciative tilts of their mouths.

"Mmm, he sure does fill out a pair of blue jeans," Sunglasses said.

Blue fanned her rosy face. "If only I were twenty years younger."

Sunglasses eyed her. "Twenty? More like forty."

"I'm a cougar," Blue shot back. "Isn't that what the kids say nowadays?"

I sputtered into my hand, nearly choking.

Blue nodded at me. "You should get busy there, dear. He won't stay single forever."

I put my hand up. "Oh no, no, he's *so* not my type."

"What? You don't like handsome, rugged men with an air of authority?" Sunglasses actually shot me that *gurrrl* look that Ginny always gave me when she thought I was full of crap.

"I do. It's just, um, the sheriff and I don't, uh, mesh well."

"You're a pretty girl. He's a handsome boy," Blue said. "What else is there to mesh?"

"Well, I kind of would like to actually *like* the man I want to mesh with."

Blue waved her wrinkled, ring-laden hand at me. "That's so overrated. Passion is where it's at."

Sunglasses nodded in agreement. "Amen, sister."

I looked toward the house and noticed that Sheriff Jackson had already gone inside. After what the ladies had told me, I had a fleeting thought that maybe I had made a mistake in calling the sheriff. If what they said was true about Mrs. Walker and her treatment of Lulu, maybe Mr. Rainer had actually rescued the dog from a horrible situation. I didn't necessarily agree with the action, but I definitely sympathized with the motive. In similar circumstances, I may have done the same thing. My cats, Scout and Jem, were both rescues. If anyone ever mistreated them, that person would be in a world of hurt.

The gals were chatting away beside me; I didn't think they even noticed I wasn't listening. Not until something Blue said drew my attention back to them.

"I'm sorry…what did you just say?"

"That her great-nephew, Peter, did everything for that woman, and she treated him like a servant."

I shook my head. "No, you said something about Peter's wife, Colleen Walker."

"Now there's a woman just as cranky as Ida," Sunglasses said.

"So true," Blue agreed. "She never waves hello when she's here. Didn't even acknowledge me this morning. And I was out in the yard plain as day, smiling at her while I watered the roses."

"You saw Colleen this morning?" I asked.

Blue nodded. "Yes, it's Tuesday. She checks in on Ida every Tuesday and Friday mornings."

"What time?"

She pursed her already puckered lips. "I'd say mid-morning."

"It's was around eleven," Sunglasses added, "because Ellen was on."

"Oh, that's right." Blue nodded.

This was getting more complicated as the day progressed. If Colleen was indeed in Mrs. Walker's home around eleven, that meant she was there very close to the time of death.

When I discovered her at the bottom of the stairs, Mrs. Walker hadn't been dead too long. I needed to share this info with the sheriff—pronto. I had learned from last time that withholding information and evidence would only get me into some serious trouble with him. I didn't want to go through anything like that again.

Before I could ask any more questions, Daisy joined our little neighborhood powwow. She'd ridden her bicycle here from the kennel. I made a mental note to offer her a ride back to the kennel in the golf cart. We could strap the bike on the back, no problem.

"Hey," she said as she stood beside me and looked up toward the Rainer house. "Interesting turn of events."

"Yeah, after what you'd told me, I was beyond shocked to see Lulu happily in his house."

She shook her head. "I'm having a hard time believing it."

I leaned in closer to her. "These ladies have been telling me that Mrs. Walker wasn't nice to her dog."

She scrunched up her face. "Maybe. I never saw it. If I had, I would've done something about it."

The door to the Rainer house opened, and Sheriff Jackson walked out, carrying Lulu under his arm. Mr. Rainer followed him out. He was wringing his hands and looking extremely distraught. My stomach clenched. If I'd had any doubts about how Mr. Rainer felt about the dog, they completely vanished.

"She likes to be scratched on the belly," Mr. Rainer said as he trailed after the sheriff down the porch steps to the front lawn. "And she only likes bacon treats—not the hard ones, the soft ones. The hard ones hurt her teeth."

"Okay, Mr. Rainer."

Daisy met them halfway. The sheriff handed Lulu to her. She petted the little dog's head gently. "She'll be well looked after, Mr. Rainer. I have a bunch of nice pups she can play with."

Chewing on his bottom lip, he nodded. "When do you think I can have her back?" he asked the sheriff.

"I don't know, Mr. Rainer. It's going to be up to the next of kin."

He snarled. "That Peter couldn't take care of a pet rock, let alone a precious dog like Lulu."

"I'm sorry," the sheriff said, "but you'll just have to wait and see how this plays out. Daisy will look after her until we can get it all sorted."

Mr. Rainer nodded, then he looked over at me as I waited on the sidewalk in front of the house. His glare sent a shiver down my back. "You should've kept your nose out of my business." He turned to go back into his house, mumbling the rest of that statement. I could hear "girl," "stupid," and a curse word in there somewhere.

Daisy gave me an apologetic look.

"I can drive you back to the kennels," I offered.

The sheriff stepped in the way. "I'll drive Daisy back. I need to fill out some forms for her."

"Oh, okay."

"You should go back to the hotel." He tipped his hat to Blue and Sunglasses, then picked up Daisy's bike and slid it into the back of his jeep.

"I'll see you later," Daisy said, then jumped into the passenger side.

I watched as they drove away, a ball of regret in the pit of my belly. For some reason, I felt like I had done the wrong thing. Which was a new one for me. I always tried to do the right thing, no matter what. But this time, I might have screwed up.

Blue patted me on the shoulder. "Don't fret, dear. Not everyone likes a busybody."

I didn't know how to respond to that, so I didn't. The ladies ambled across the street to their house. I slid into the golf cart and drove away.

CHAPTER NINE

LOIS WAS WAITING FOR me, arms crossed, at the side entrance to the hotel. She didn't look happy to see me. I cringed. It was bad enough having Samuel on my case every day. The last thing I needed was Lois giving me a hard time, too.

"Come this way, Andi," she said as she moved away from the doorway and into a quiet alcove. I had no choice but to follow, although I felt like I was marching to the gallows or something.

She turned to face me when we were away from prying eyes and ears. "You need to be careful, Andi. Samuel is not happy that you're here. He thinks you've brought negative attention to the Park. Ginny's been running interference for you, and she's his favorite. But he won't let you damage the Park's reputation, no matter how much he loves his granddaughter."

I couldn't believe she was accusing me of causing problems for the hotel just because I'd been the one to find that body in the maintenance room by the pool. Why did everyone conveniently skip over the fact that I'd solved the murder, too? Wasn't that worth something?

I said none of that. Instead, I bit my tongue and nodded. "Of course. I don't want to cause any trouble for any of you."

"Henry's not happy with you, either," Lois said, and my jaw dropped. Henry was her dead husband. She acted like he was still living here at the Park. Several times, I'd caught her talking to him as if he were in the room with her. I knew Ginny was worried about her, and so was Eric. But right at the moment, I figured discretion was the better part of valor where Henry was concerned.

I simply nodded. "Okay, Lois. I'll do better."

"See that you do," she replied before she turned and left me standing there, wondering if she'd totally lost her mind. Did she think Henry was a ghost? Surely talking to ghosts was a sign of some level of nutty, wasn't it? I shook my head when a shiver ran over me. I needed a break, for sure.

When I got back to my suite, a postcard from San Francisco was on the floor inside my door. It must've been slipped under— someone's version of mail delivery for the staff at the hotel.

I set the letter on the table. Curious who would send me a postcard, I flipped it over. There was some Russian scrawled at the top, then it said: *Sorry I couldn't do more for you. Regards, Beatrice Sorokin.*

Beatrice Sorokin. One of the many clients of our law firm that Jeremy had bilked. She had been one of my favorites, and I'd spent a lot of extra time just chatting with her because it seemed to please her, to have someone to talk to about nothing in particular. And she had the cutest little dog, too. I was surprised but happy that she'd written to me.

I appreciated her words, but I wondered what the Russian meant. I had no idea that Beatrice was Russian. Smiling, I set the postcard on my shelf in between a photo of Miss Charlotte and one of Ginny and her family.

The Park family photo included Henry. He and Lois seemed happy in this photo, which was taken a couple of years before he died. I'd met Henry several times when I visited Ginny's home while we were in college. He'd always treated me well, and I'd liked him. He didn't look at all like his father. In this photo, though, Samuel was as dapper as ever.

I glanced briefly at the photo of my parents taken a dozen years ago. They looked happy, too. I shrugged. Photos always seemed to capture people when they were at their best. I never saw family photos where the people were angry or crying or anything.

It had been a while since I'd seen my parents. They didn't come home for my college graduation. They didn't come for my law school graduation, either. I'd been to Hong Kong a few times since they moved, but it was such an arduous trip. Once I entered law school, I'd started volunteering at the legal aid clinic, and then I'd graduated and got a job right away. Thinking back, I guess I hadn't seen them in about ten years. Hard to believe. Where does the time go?

I slapped the fish fillet into a small frying pan, seasoned it, and put it on a burner. I wasn't much of a cook, so this would be an interesting experiment. The clerk had made it sound so easy, but I couldn't bake the fish like she said. I didn't have an oven. I crossed my finger and said a quick prayer that this would work. Just in case, I took the batteries out of the smoke detector.

As I watched the fish sizzle, I thought about all the meals I'd had with Miss Charlotte. She was an amazing cook and had tried to teach me, but nothing ever stuck. I could boil eggs, make ramen noodles and a decent dressing for a salad, but beyond that,

I was lost. It wasn't that I couldn't follow a recipe. I could quite easily—I was good with directions. But I didn't understand the flavors and what spices went with what. I was completely clueless about all of that. Cooking well was more than a nuance, a desire for which I just hadn't been able to cultivate.

Of course, my mother was of no help. I was sure she had never cooked a day in her life. Even if she could've cooked, she wouldn't have bothered to teach me. I often wondered why my parents had even bothered to have me. I shrugged. Probably because having children was expected of them at the time. To fit into their small group of haughty friends. After they were offered the chance of a lifetime and moved to Hong Kong, I'm sure it was anything but convenient to have a teenager and her nanny to support back in the States.

After I flipped the fish, I made a simple green salad with raspberry vinaigrette. I put the meal on a plate and took it out onto the patio to eat. The evening was too nice to waste by staying inside. That was definitely one thing I didn't miss about my condo in California: the view. There, all I could see from the patio was the condo building next door and the tiny green space between them. Here, it was all big blue sky, green cliffs, and the expanse of the turbulent Lake Michigan beyond.

I took a deep breath of cool, fresh April air and smiled. This was all pretty awesome right now. I took a bite of fish, surprised that it tasted good enough to eat, and looked out over the hotel grounds. I had a decent job, a nice place to live, and my best friend Ginny to lean on when I needed to. I missed my cats, though. Having them with me would have made my room perfect. I had trouble sleeping without them nearby.

Maybe it was time I started thinking seriously about getting a place in the village. Rent might not be too high. Not like in

California. My place there had cost thirty-five hundred a month, and that had been the rate for the past two years. I'd ask Ginny about moving out of the hotel soon. Maybe she'd have some suggestions.

I glanced at the framed photos again. Mom and Dad were standing together at the entrance to Club Paradise. The building was impressive enough, and the interior was even more lavish. They'd been offered the opportunity to manage the club originally. When the owner died, they'd bought the club from the family. One of the reasons they rarely came back to see me, they said, were the demands of running an exclusive private club across the globe. I'd always felt they were making excuses. But now that I'd been living and working at the Park, I had a better appreciation for the challenges my parents, Drew and Emily, must face, too.

I glanced at my phone on the coffee table. I felt like it was challenging me. I studied it a few seconds while I chewed and swallowed. Oh, why not? I'd need to talk to them sooner or later, anyway. I took a deep breath, hit the speaker button, and placed the call. It took a few moments to connect before I heard the ringing sounds. They were a bit delayed. After the tenth ring, I was surprised to notice how disappointed I felt as the call flipped over to voice mail.

I cleared my throat. "Hi, Mom. Dad. I'm having dinner and called to catch up. You must be busy. Call when you can." I paused half a moment before I added a quick and breezy, "Love you." I disconnected the call and tossed the phone aside.

While I was finishing the last bite of my meal, there was a knock on my door. I went to answer it and found Lane from the front reception standing there with a giant bouquet of flowers.

"Hey, Andi. Special delivery for you."

I opened the door, and he carried the lavender vase of pink and purple flowers in and set them on my coffee table. The arrangement matched the décor of my suite.

"Wow, these are gorgeous. Who are they from?"

He made a face. "Don't know. June's delivery guy, Todd, brought them to the front for you."

I frowned. "Does Todd work at the D&W as well?"

"I have no idea." He shrugged. "I'll see you later."

"Okay, thanks."

He went to the door and let himself out.

I grabbed the small white card nestled inside the flowers. It read, "Thinking about you." No name. I bent forward and inhaled the rich aroma of the pink lilies and purple violets. Whoever sent these had to have known I had a weakness for those two flowers. Were they from the handsome mayor of Frontenac City? Daniel could easily have weaseled my flower preferences out of Ginny.

Setting the card down on the table, I grabbed my purse and rummaged inside my wallet for Daniel's business card. I fiddled with it for a minute, staring at the phone numbers, wondering if I should call him. But what if the flowers weren't from him? Then I'd look like a fool. A desperate one at that.

I tossed the business card on the table, not one hundred percent sure I wanted to risk it. I took another sniff of the flowers and sighed. They were beautiful, whoever sent them.

Another knock at my door. Ginny walked in, fully glammed up. She had the best eyeliner skills. I could never get it right. I always ended up looking like an Egyptian at Halloween.

"Ready to go?" she asked.

"Um, go where?"

"To the bar. It's our girls' night out, remember?"

"Ginny, I—"

She spotted the flowers and grinned. "Oh my God, who sent you these?" She smelled them, then grabbed the little notecard and read it. "A secret admirer?"

"I don't know."

"Maybe Daniel?"

I shrugged, not wanting her to know how much I wanted the sender to be Daniel. "Maybe."

"Sheriff Jackson?"

I frowned. "Why on earth would the sheriff send me flowers?"

She made a face. "I don't know. I'm just tossing out the names of the men in your life. It's a pretty short list." She snorted out a laugh in her adorable way.

"The sheriff would most definitely not send me flowers. Not even if I was laid up in the hospital. Probably not even to my funeral."

"Well, whoever it was spent a pretty penny. Arrangements like these are not cheap." She smelled the flowers again and then regarded me. "You don't look like you're ready to go out."

"I'm not sure—"

"You're going. Period. There is no argument you can make, Counselor, that would deter me from forcing you to come to the bar with me for a few drinks."

I looked at her eager face and relented. "Fine."

"Yay!" She clapped her hands. "So, let's get you ready."

I glanced down at the simple slacks and blouse I was wearing. "What's wrong with what I have on?"

"We don't have that kind of time. So, I'll just help you out." She went up the steps to my bedroom and opened the wardrobe. She pulled out a cute, short, flowered dress that I was saving for a special occasion. "This will do."

A half hour later, I was expertly made up. My makeup was understated but did amazing things to my eyes and cheekbones. Ginny had twisted my hair into a messy bun, with a few tendrils framing my face. She said the look was like catnip to guys who would want desperately to tuck those stray hairs behind my ears. No wonder she had so many dates. She had flirtation down to a science.

CHAPTER TEN

WE WALKED DOWN TO the village. It wasn't far, maybe fifteen minutes. Ginny wanted to go to the Swan Song, which was at the far end of Main Street. She claimed there was "better clientele" there than at the Victoria, which was across the street from Daisy's place. What she really meant was there were younger men at the Swan. The median age at the Victoria was likely around fifty. It didn't matter to me, as I had no intention of flirting with anyone.

The walk down Main was always pleasant. It was a great place to people watch—this was where most of the tourists congregated—and an opportunity to window shop. Now that my bank account was slightly healthier, I wanted to buy some new shoes. The last three pair were ruined by circumstances beyond my control. My body did a little quiver just thinking about the last one. Watching a screaming woman I barely knew give birth was not my idea of a good time.

I stopped at several boutiques along the way, ignoring Ginny's urgency to get to the Swan. First stop was Envy, which was a high-end dress shop. It's where I had sent a mother of the bride-to-be recently when she had ruined her dress. They had some great dresses and cute shoes, but nothing jumped out at me. Next up was Color Me Red. There were a lot of flowy, gauzy blouses and shifts on the racks. Jasmine incense burned on the front counter, filling up the shop with a light, flowery scent. I had a feeling Ginny shopped here often. When we walked in, both clerks screamed her name and gave her a hug. All I found on the shoe racks were platforms and ballet flats, neither of which would work very well for a concierge who spends her days on her feet.

The final store was called Blossom Boutique. The décor was Victorian and rustic. Lots of pink and frills on the walls and tables. Along one wall were shelves of shoes, and I found the perfect pair of strappy white sandals. Snagged my size, bought them. It was the first extravagant purchase I'd made in a long time. It felt good to have the cash to pay for it. I was starting to feel like my old self again. Strong and independent.

With my new purchase in a cute pink paper bag, I followed Ginny into the Swan. I'd been here once before, nosing around…well, asking about a potential witness and whether she had worked here or not. So I really didn't get a chance to absorb the full experience. It was definitely lively, lots of happy people jammed together in two small rooms. We pushed our way slowly to the bar because Ginny got stopped now and then by different patrons, and ordered drinks. A Guinness for Ginny and a lemon drop martini garnished with a tiny yellow rose for me.

Drinks in hand, we made our way to the far side of the bar where Ginny spied a table in the corner. We sat, clinked glasses, and took a much-needed sip of our respective drinks. I actually sighed.

"You see," Ginny said, "you needed this."

"I did. Thank you." I took another sip, relishing the warmth that spread over my limbs. It had been a long while since I'd enjoyed a nice quiet drink, and I worried—a little— that the alcohol would hit me hard. But right now, I didn't care. I just wanted to relax and savor this moment with my best friend.

We chatted about everything and anything. It was nice to not have to think about my legal issues, my job problems, or how I'd just happened to come across another dead body in such a short span of time. Ginny made me laugh, and by the time I finished my martini, I was feeling light and floaty.

"Should we have another?" Ginny asked, already getting to her feet to walk over to the bar.

"Why not?"

Two full glasses—one a beer and the other a martini—were suddenly plunked down onto our table. I looked up to see Clinton, one of the guys who had installed a new patio door for me when someone had thrown a rock through the glass. This was during the first murder scandal.

"Here you go, ladies," he said cheerfully.

Ginny's grin was huge. "Clinton! I didn't know you'd be here."

But I suspected that wasn't true and she'd known exactly when Clinton would be there. That's why she'd insisted on this pub, at this time. I should have known.

But I didn't mind. Ginny positively glowed as she chatted with him. Who was I to interfere with that? She deserved to find love. In the past, she'd had a bad run with men. They never seemed to treat her very well. It made me sad when she always blamed herself for the failing relationships when she simply had an unfortunate talent for choosing the wrong men.

I happily sipped on my second martini as Ginny flirted with Clinton. I loved that he made her giggle and she'd lightly touch his arm. I had a feeling that I was going to be walking back to the hotel alone.

A man slid into the chair beside me, and I turned to see Karl Neumann, brother to Dr. Neumann, making himself comfortable on my left. "It's Andi, right?"

"It is. And you're Karl."

"Guilty as charged."

"Did you get your place all fixed?"

"I did." He laughed. "Thanks for remembering."

"Kind of hard to forget." It seemed like only yesterday—I'd witnessed him during a fistfight that had damaged his apartment and ended in a parking lot.

"Can I buy you another drink to thank you for stopping Nathan from pounding the ever-loving snot out of me?"

I laughed and pointed toward my nearly full martini. "No, but thanks. Two's my limit. I'm good."

"Some other time, maybe?"

"Maybe."

He tipped his head to me then headed to the bar, sliding onto a stool next to a pretty brunette in short shorts and a tank top. I thought I recognized her but couldn't put my finger on exactly where I'd seen her before. Must have been the alcohol clouding my brain. Which meant it was time to get some sleep.

I grabbed Ginny's hand. "I'm going home."

"No, stay for one more."

"I've had enough. I've got to work tomorrow, you know." I glanced at Clinton; he only had eyes for Ginny. "You two enjoy yourselves."

"I can come with you."

I shook my head. "No, I'm fine to walk back on my own. It's not even that dark out."

"Only if you're sure."

"I am." Standing, I bent down and kissed her forehead. "Be safe."

"You, too."

I grabbed my shoe bag and made my way outside. I took in a deep breath and smiled. I would never get tired of that refreshing lake scent. It filled me with a joy I hadn't even realized I was missing.

Wrapping my arms around myself to ward off a little chill, I started the walk back to the hotel. The streets were still hopping with locals and tourists. There were several restaurants and entertainment establishments along Main Street that were filled to the brim. The sounds of music and laughter spilled out onto the street.

I was just past the Frontenac Island Bubbles Soap Company when my cell phone buzzed. I pulled it out of my purse and looked at the caller ID. Unknown. I answered anyway. Two lemon drop martinis, and I was already throwing caution to the wind.

"Hello?"

At first, I thought the caller had hung up. All I heard was dead air. But then the faint exhalation of breath caught my ear, and I took a wild guess at the nature of the call.

"Seriously?" I said. "Do desperate man-boys still make obscene phone calls nowadays?"

"Been thinking about you, Andi."

Then he disconnected.

I froze on the sidewalk and looked around. Was I being watched? The call unnerved me, and I thought about turning down the next street and going to the sheriff's station. But I shook that thought away. It was nothing. Just some dude being a jerk. I wasn't in any danger.

Or maybe I was lying to myself.

As I walked quickly up the road, my gaze darted into the creeping shadows along the buildings and back alleys as a precaution. I had no idea what I'd do if someone attacked me.

CHAPTER ELEVEN

"GOOD MORNING," I SAID to the twentysomething brunette woman in big, dark sunglasses leaning on the concierge desk. "How may I help you today?"

"Well," she took off her sunglasses and smiled. Her eyes were a bit glassy. She'd obviously had a wild evening. "I'm getting married."

"Congratulations, Miss...?"

"Melanie Lawson."

I did some fast typing into my computer and found her room number. I narrowed my eyes at her. I recognized her from the pub last night. She had been seated at the bar alone for a while until Karl Neumann slid onto the stool beside her.

I also recognized her from when she checked in with three other young women yesterday. They were on some kind of after-college party, they'd said. I didn't remember any mention of a wedding, and her parents were VIPs at the Park. Because of their stature, I was sure I'd have heard a lot more about her wedding long before now. "When is the big day?"

"That's where you come in," she said.

I stared at her, wide-eyed in anticipation, waiting for the punchline because I knew there was going to be one.

"I want to get married tonight."

And there it was.

"I see." I smiled, stalling. "And you want to get married here. At the hotel."

She nodded. "Yeah, in the maze."

I tried to keep my eyebrows from rising with concern, but they had a mind of their own and sometimes acted independently. My voice clicked up an octave. "In the hedge maze in our garden?"

She nodded again, even more enthusiastically this time. "It will be so cool. I'll come in from one end, and he'll come in from the other, and we'll meet in the middle at the gazebo and say our vows. It's totally going to be video recorded, and I'll post it on my Instagram." She leaned further over the counter as if she wanted to share a secret with me. "I have over one hundred thousand followers. I'm kind of a big deal."

"I'm sure you are." I didn't let my smile waver, especially since Samuel was hovering around nearby. I didn't see him, but I could sense his presence. A VIP's daughter wanted a flash wedding at the Park. It was the kind of thing Samuel would demand to be informed about. "So, I imagine you'll be needing a dress? And bridesmaid dresses?"

"Yes, and they need to be old-timey."

"Old-timey?"

"Yeah, like from the 1800s or something like that."

"Is that a personal preference, or is there some significance I should know?"

"My man is totally into old stuff. He's like some historian or something. Real smart-like."

It was all starting to dawn on me, and I didn't like where this was going. "What is your fiancé's name?"

"Karl Neumann. Do you know him?"

I clenched my jaw, trying not to let my mouth fall open in disbelief. "Yes, I know Karl."

"He's awesome, isn't he?"

How should I respond to that? I cleared my throat to avoid choking. "Oh yes, he's something all right."

"So, can this all happen, or what? You can charge everything to the room. My parents will pay."

"I will certainly do my best for you, Miss Lawson." I glanced up to see Samuel openly watching me now from twenty feet away so he could hear the conversation as well. I slid a pen and pad of paper over to her. "If you could just give me your cell phone number and tell me your size, and how many bridesmaids and their sizes. I'm sure I can find you some exquisite dresses for the wedding."

She eagerly jotted down the information. "Oh my God, you are totally the best. I'm going to leave you a huge tip when I check out."

Once I had all the information I needed, I sent her on her way with a promise to call her once I had the dresses and the wedding nuptials organized. I also needed to call a justice of the peace and book the garden maze for a few hours.

As soon as she left, Samuel approached my desk. "What was that all about?"

"Melanie Lawson. She's getting married here. Tonight, she says."

He gave me the usual stink eye. "Where are her parents?"

I shrugged. "I don't know. They haven't checked in, have they?"

He turned on his heel and left without another word.

I was definitely going to need help with this one. For more than one reason.

First, I called Ginny. "I need to see you ASAP."

Ten minutes later, she crossed the busy lobby from the offices and came up to the desk. "What's up?"

"I need to plan a wedding. To take place in seven hours."

"For who?"

"One of the guests. Melanie Lawson."

Her eyes went wide. "No way-ay! I know the Lawson family. They come here often. They are, like, uber rich. Why didn't they let us know? A Lawson wedding will be big, big news here and everywhere. Who is she marrying?"

"Karl Neumann."

Now her jaw dropped open. Gaping mouth, wide eyes, the whole bit. She didn't say anything for a second or two, then the delayed response fairly leapt from her mouth. "What? You're kidding!"

"Nope, that's what she told me."

"No way. Karl is not engaged. That news would've been the talk of the town."

I made a face. "I think maybe they just met last night."

"What?!" Her voice went up a few octaves. "Oh, my God!"

People turned to look at us. Lane at the front reception desk frowned, as did Samuel, who was standing nearby with a cell phone held to his ear. He was probably calling the Lawsons right that very minute.

I just knew he was still lurking.

"Keep your voice down," I said.

"Sorry. It's just…what the hell?"

"I saw her last night at the bar, and I saw Karl hit on her. You were talking to Clinton."

"Unbelievable. There is no way her parents are going to agree to this." She shook her head. "What are you going to do? Are you going to plan the wedding?"

"Well, she's legally an adult, old enough to make her own decisions. And she is a guest and I am the concierge, and according to your grandpa, I should do everything in my power to help the guests no matter what."

"Andi…if this backfires and the Lawsons cause a stink, which they will, you're done here. Samuel will be livid. Lois, too, for that matter. You know that, right?"

"Why does everything blow back on me? I was just standing here, minding my own business, when Melanie Lawson dropped this bomb in my lap. How is that my fault?" I gave her a look. But she was genuinely horrified about the wedding, so I knocked my indignation down a couple of notches. "What do you take me for? Of course I'm going to go into town and have a little chat with Karl, on the pretense of finding Melanie and her bridesmaids the perfect old-timey dresses."

She practically sighed with relief and patted my arm. "I knew you would do the right thing."

"So, how was *your* last night?"

Ginny blushed. "Good."

"How good?" She blushed harder, and I shook my head. She cleared her throat. "Did you get back okay?"

"Yeah, the walk was pleasant and uneventful." I kept the anonymous creepy phone call to myself. I didn't want to worry her. Also, I didn't want to admit that I had almost jogged all the way back to the hotel. Or that I had dead-bolted the lock on my door and made sure my patio door was secure. And certainly not that I had slept with all the lights on all night.

CHAPTER TWELVE

AN HOUR LATER, I was heading down to the village—to the historical society, specifically. I hoped I could find Karl and find out exactly what the heck was going on. When I reached the old stone building, I saw that the door was shut, and there was a sign that read: *Be back in ten minutes*. I tried the handle and found it was locked up tight. I went around back to the stairs that led up to Karl's apartment, which was on the second floor.

I knocked on his door a few times, but there was no answer. I pressed my face to the window next to the door just in case. The last time I came looking for Karl, his place had been trashed, and he was getting his face punched by a vengeful husband. His place didn't look trashed this time. It looked like the ordinary amount of bachelor messy.

I walked back down Market Street, not sure where to start my search for Karl. I didn't really know him. I had no idea where his usual haunts were. Who could I ask for that information? I stopped in front of the sheriff's office and realized I had my own personal information booth right there.

I went inside. Deputy Shawn, as usual, was manning the front desk. He smiled when he saw me this time. It was a far cry from the condescending smirk I usually got.

"Hello, Andi."

"Deputy."

"Looking for the sheriff, I imagine." Before I could answer, he opened the half door so I could come inside. I did, not wanting to look a gift horse in the mouth, which I'd been told was bad luck. "He's in his office."

I knocked briefly on the glass door and got a gruff, "Come in."

Sheriff Jackson leaned forward in his chair and flopped his hands onto his desk in defeat before I said a single word. I smiled at my small triumph. "What do you need, Andi?"

I sat in the visitor's chair. "I'm looking for Karl Neumann."

His eyes narrowed. "You think Karl had something to do with Mrs. Walker's death?"

"What? No." I waved my hand at him before the implication settled. When it dawned, I replied, "So, you don't think her death was an accident, then, do you?"

He leaned back in his chair and rubbed at his chin. "There were some inconsistencies in the postmortem with how she fell."

I gaped at him. I couldn't believe he offered up that information so freely.

He must've read the look on my face. "I figure letting you know is easier than having to put you in check all the darn time."

I tried to cover the smile that blossomed on my face, but failed.

"Don't look so smug."

"I'm not smug."

His eyebrow came up at that.

"Okay, maybe a little smug. I'm just so glad you realized how easy it is to share with me, that you know how much of an asset I can be."

He came forward in his chair. "I never said that."

"What about Mr. Rainer?" The old guy had stolen Mrs. Walker's dog, after all. Who knew what else he might have done?

"He has an alibi. Cleaning woman was in his house from eight in the morning until noon."

Now that I was in a more generous mood toward the sheriff, I offered him a tidbit, too. "Did you know Colleen Walker visited Mrs. Walker that morning?"

"I didn't. We haven't had a chance to talk to Colleen. Talked to Peter, and he never mentioned that."

I beamed. I had supplied information that he didn't already have. Perhaps he'd be a little grateful. "I also heard Colleen on the phone that day, and she didn't sound too broken up about Ida's death."

"Noted."

"Did you talk with whoever delivered the groceries? Probably the D&W delivery kid, Todd, if I had to bet."

His eyes narrowed. "You are informed, aren't you?"

"I'm naturally inquisitive. My nanny used to call me Miss Kitty sometimes. Because cats are naturally curious, too." *Not sure why I told him that.*

"Yeah, I talked to Todd. He said he delivered the groceries and then left. He said he normally puts the groceries away, but he was in a rush and couldn't do it that day. The cashier, Hannah, backs his story."

I thought about Todd's agitation while he had been on the phone in the parking lot at the market, but kept it to myself for now. Maybe that had nothing to do with Mrs. Walker. It could have been simply a spat with his girlfriend, which was the vibe I got at the time.

"If I hear of anything, I'll let you know," the sheriff said.

"I appreciate that. You see how easy it is to work together?" I smiled.

He just nodded and made some kind of guttural noise in his throat.

I got to my feet. "I'll be going now."

"Didn't you want to know about Karl Neumann's whereabouts?" he asked.

"Oh, yes. Right. I do."

"He's not at the historical society or his place?"

I shook my head. "Not sure where else I could look for him. It's kind of an emergency."

"Try the Swan or the calzone place on Main. He goes there for lunch most days, and I'm pretty sure he's sleeping with the girl who works there." He shook his head. "Not sure where that guy finds the time for all his women."

"Thanks, Sheriff." I went to the door but stopped. "Do you like lilies?"

He frowned. "Like the flower?"

"Yeah."

"Uh, I guess. I don't know. They're flowers. They smell nice sometimes."

I gave him a thumbs-up. "I'll let you get back to it. Have a good day."

When I walked out of the station, I almost tripped over a young woman sitting on the ground in front of the door, smoking a cigarette. I was about to say something impolite, but then I recognized her. She was a coworker. One of the hotel's cleaning staff.

"Megan?"

She looked up at me, her hair in her face, but I could still see the salty tear streaks on her cheeks. "Hey." She wiped at her nose with the back of her hand.

"Are you okay?"

She nodded.

"Are you sure? You don't look okay."

She got to her feet as more tears rolled down from her eyes. "Patrick broke up with me."

"Oh. I'm sorry to hear that." I wasn't the least bit sorry, because Patrick wasn't a good match for her. He was ten years older, and he didn't seem like a great guy based on the encounters I'd had with him a few times at the hotel's restaurant.

She sniffed and wiped her nose with her sleeve. "He said I was too immature for him."

I nodded, partly because Patrick was right. "It's probably for the best, Megan. You can do a lot better."

"But he said he loved me, when we...when we..."

She didn't need to finish that sentence. I knew exactly the type of situation she was talking about. "Oh, honey." I opened my arms, and she came into them willingly.

She sobbed as I patted her back. Sometimes it was so hard being a girl. Crap like this made me want to kick every guy in the crotch. Especially a guy like Patrick, who was definitely old enough to know better. A lot of guys weren't careless like that with a girl's emotions, but I was sure every woman on earth had suffered through something similar or knew someone who had.

I let her cry it out as I made comforting humming noises. I should've probably offered some wise words, but I couldn't come up with any. My personal experiences didn't start at such a young age. By the time I was dealing with guys and sex, I was out on my own, living in a dorm. Miss Charlotte was long gone back to her home in Texas. Anyway, sometimes all a girl needed was a hug.

Once Megan's tears dried up, she pulled away a little. I rummaged in my purse for tissues and handed the packet to her.

"Thanks," she said.

"No problem. We Park Hotel women have to stick together."

The door to the station opened, and the sheriff came out. He pulled up short when he saw his daughter wiping her eyes, and me standing near her.

"What's going on?"

Megan shook her head. "Nothing. Just hotel business."

He regarded me, as if I would reveal the truth. But there were some secrets in this town that Sheriff Jackson didn't need to know. Megan was his daughter, but she wasn't a child anymore. She'd have to come clean with him if she wanted him to know—it wasn't up to me to spill that particular can of worms.

Megan turned and hugged me again. "Thank you, Andi."

I patted her shoulder. "Anytime, kiddo."

She looked at her dad. "Ready for lunch?"

He nodded, seeming a bit flustered at what had just transpired. Poor guy. I imagined raising a daughter on his own had been challenging since his ex left town.

Megan bounced down the steps to the sidewalk, texting on her phone as she did.

The sheriff glanced at me. "Is there something I should know?"

Smiling, I patted him on the shoulder, too. "I'd tell you if there was. You know that, right?"

He gave me a blank look and then joined his daughter.

CHAPTER THIRTEEN

UPON MY RETURN TO the hotel's concierge desk, after an hour's fruitless search for Karl, I found Casey Cushing and Samuel being all buddy-buddy nearby. Casey gave me a warm, friendly smile as I slid behind the large wooden desk, and I returned it. But I could feel the knife being jammed in my back from across the room.

Trying hard not to look over as the two of them laughed and joked like old friends, I found Karl's number in the hotel's business directory and called it. He didn't answer, so I left a message.

"Hi, Karl. This is Andi from the Park Hotel. We have some urgent business to discuss with you. Please return my call as soon as possible."

I had a sneaky suspicion that good old Karl was lying low. Hiding from his future bride. Hiding from the ridiculous decision he'd made last night, likely induced by copious amounts of alcohol and sex. Because of this, I didn't know what to do about planning the wedding. It was my job to make sure every guest was fully satisfied and got even more than what they requested, but this one just didn't feel right.

I called Ginny to get some clarity. She was the events manager at the hotel, after all.

"So, I searched for Karl but couldn't find him. I have a feeling I'm not going to find him within the next twelve hours. I'm not sure what to do in this situation."

"Well, technically, Melanie is an adult and able to make her own decisions, as you said earlier. However bad they may be."

"I know."

"I think you've made a valiant effort to find out what's going on. No one will fault you on that."

"You think I should just go ahead and do what she's asked for? Get the wedding set up for tonight in the maze?"

"Yeah. Her crappy decision is not worth your job."

"You think my job's in jeopardy?"

"I never said that."

"But you implied it." I glanced over at Samuel as he slapped a hand on Casey's back and laughed at something he said. "Samuel's looking for an excuse to fire me, isn't he?"

There was a long pause that I didn't like. "No. You're fine. Just keep doing a good job, and you'll be okay."

"Do you think I'm doing a good job? Be honest."

"Yes. I do. Quit worrying."

"Okay. Then can you book the garden and maze for me tonight from six to nine?"

"Done."

"Thanks, Ginny."

After I hung up with her, I called June to order some flowers and a bouquet for the bride. I made sure to tell June to make an arrangement reminiscent of the late 1800s. I was sure she would know what that would be. June seemed like a woman who knew all kinds of things.

Now I needed to get something arranged for food and drinks for the small reception. Since the wedding was to be at night in the garden with an 1800s theme, I thought tea, cucumber sandwiches, and some kind of little pastries would do the trick for starters. I'd leave the full menu plan up to Justin. He was the chef and would know what he could put together on short notice. I'd also have to phone around to the cake shops for a wedding cake unless he could whip up something suitable.

Before I could pick up the phone to make those calls, Casey sidled up to the desk and leaned on the counter. "How are you today, Andi?"

"I'm good, thank you, Casey. And you? How is your mother?"

"Oh, I'm terrific, and Mom is doing very well. In fact, the doctors say she won't be bedridden for as long as they first thought. She's healing very quickly."

"That's great to hear," I lied. My stomach started churning. How long could I count on this job if Casey wanted it back? And if I got fired, where would I go? Ginny had been my last resort, and this place was the end of the line.

"It is. Her doctors said originally that it would be six to eight months for a full recovery, but it could be quicker."

"I'm so glad." I tried to keep the sarcasm out of my voice. It wasn't that I didn't want Mrs. Cushing to recover. I did. I had no ill will toward the woman. From what I'd heard about her, she was a very pleasant and friendly person.

It was her son that I had a problem with. He wasn't the charming, good-natured man everyone saw. There was a bit of a jerk deep down inside. A conniving, manipulative jerk. I just knew it. I'd seen his kind before. My old boss Jeremy had been the poster boy, and look what happened there.

Casey leaned closer to me, sure that I was the only one that could hear what he was about to say. "So, just a heads-up about not getting too cozy in my job. I will be back sooner rather than later. Samuel will be ecstatic to have me back. He said that exact thing just a few minutes ago. In fact, he says it every time I see him. Which is often, since he and my mother are friends."

I kept the toothy grin on my face as Samuel walked up to the desk alongside Casey. "Are you ready for a round of golf, my boy?"

"Yes, sir, I am. Been looking forward to this all week."

Samuel slapped him on the back. "Me, too."

Casey finger-waved at me as the two of them walked out of the hotel and headed toward the clubhouse.

I must've had some weird look on my face because Ginny's brother, Eric, crossed the lobby toward me. He hadn't said much to me at all since I'd arrived on the island. In fact, he went out of his way to avoid me as much as possible. Probably because he didn't want his wife to be any more upset about my being here than she already was.

"Are you okay?" he asked.

I nodded and then rubbed at my jawline. Pain radiated there. I must've been clenching my teeth to stop me from saying what I really wanted to say to both Casey and Samuel.

"I'm sorry Samuel is putting you through the wringer."

"Oh, you've noticed?"

He nodded. "I think everyone's noticed. He isn't one for subtlety."

"Why does he dislike me so much?"

"I don't think it's that. I just think he hates change." Eric paused, as if he was deciding how much to reveal about his family. "After Dad died, Grandpa really fought against any kind of change here. It took forever for him to agree that Mom could run the hotel. It was more than a year before he trusted her enough to leave the island at all, even for a few hours."

I skipped over my concerns about Lois's fitness for managing the place and nodded. "Yeah, I'm thinking I don't have forever to convince him I'm a valuable member of the team, either. More valuable than Casey, I mean."

He scrunched up his face and looked away.

"What?"

"What, what?" he said.

"You made a face. I know that face. It says, 'Girl, you have no idea.'"

"Samuel's been making phone calls to California," he said with a grimace.

My stomach felt like it fell to the floor. "About me?"

"Yeah. I'm pretty sure he talked to the remaining partners at your former firm."

"Great." I threw up my hands. "I can just imagine the kind of crap they've told him."

"For what it's worth, I think Sam's wrong. I think you're very trustworthy and a good representative for the hotel. The guests like you."

"Really?" I smiled at him. Eric had no idea how much that meant to me. I'd always respected Eric and valued his opinions. "That means a lot, Eric. I can't express how much." I laid my hand on top of his and squeezed.

He looked down at our joined hands and smiled.

"You have got to be kidding me!"

We both looked over to see his wife, Nicole, frozen in her spot in the lobby, glaring at us.

Oops.

I snatched my hand back, but it was too late. The damage had already been done.

Nicole spun on her heel and marched toward the restaurant. If I could've seen her face, smoke was probably billowing out of her nose and both ears, too.

"Damn it." Eric turned to follow her, but I stopped him.

"Let me do it. I think it's time for us to have a chat. She's been silently—well, maybe not so silently—hating on me since I arrived. It can't go on any longer. She has to know for certain that there is absolutely nothing between you and me."

He nodded. "Right. Yeah, that's probably a good idea. Clear the air. Get the truth out in the open."

My eyes narrowed as I regarded him. "There's really not much to get out in the open, Eric. We went out one time, and nothing happened."

"Yeah, I know. That's what I meant."

Not completely sure that Eric agreed with me about there being nothing between us, I marched into the restaurant to track down Nicole. I assumed she was headed toward her office in the back. I passed Colleen Walker on the way through the kitchen. She was getting ready for the supper rush and didn't even glance my way.

Nicole's office door was shut. She'd probably slammed it in her fit of pique. I knocked once briskly, opened the door, and went in. I knew if I waited for a jovial "come in," I'd be standing outside until hell froze over.

"What do you want?" She glared at me from behind the desk.

"To talk."

"Why? So you can tell me that my husband is still in love with you?"

I slid into the hard wooden visitor's chair. "What? That's stupid. Eric has never been in love with me. We were friends. We went out on one date a zillion years ago. Nothing happened between us. I'm pretty sure we laughed through the goodnight cheek-to-cheek air kiss."

Nicole's eyes narrowed. "That's not how I heard it. From what Eric told me, and how messed up he was when I met him, you nearly destroyed him."

"Well, I can't help what Eric may have told you in the past. What I'm telling you now is the truth. There was nothing between Eric and me back then, and there certainly isn't anything going on now. For everyone's sake, accept that and move on." Then I threw in a slightly too obsequious, "Please?"

She worried at her bottom lip as she thought about what I'd said. I could see in her eyes that she wanted to believe me. She leaned forward in her chair and was about to say something when shouting in the kitchen interrupted us.

"What the hell?" Nicole jumped up from her chair and came around the desk to the door.

I stopped her before she could walk out. I opened the door a crack and put my finger to my lips to tell her to be quiet. I pulled her in next to me so I could see the scene playing out.

Colleen was in the kitchen with a tall man, who I assumed was her husband Peter. He was clearly angry. His hands were fisted at his sides, and his cheeks flushed a bit ruddy.

"What did you do, Colleen?"

"I don't know what you're talking about."

"Aunt Ida was right about you. You're nothing but a money-hungry bit—"

Colleen slapped him across the face. The crack reverberated through the kitchen. "You hated her just as much as I did. You would've done the same thing."

I came out of the office. The argument was obviously getting out of hand. "Okay, you two need to calm down. This isn't the place."

"Who the hell are you?" Peter glared at me.

"Andi Steele. I'm the concierge here. I'm also the one who found your aunt's body."

His face changed then. There was still a lot of rage, but I thought I could see some regret, maybe even grief. Maybe he cared more than he let on. I didn't think anyone could take care of another human being and not have feelings about them. Even if the woman was the most cantankerous person ever to exist, which was what I was starting to piece together from various accounts of Mrs. Walker.

"Stay out of this, Andi," Colleen snarled, "Mind your own business." Like a raging bull, she actually came at me. I stood my ground. She stopped mere inches from my face. "I saw you following me the other day. Sticking your nose in where it doesn't belong."

Nicole stepped out in front of me. "Stop, Colleen. Don't make this worse. I will call the sheriff."

Colleen paused, maybe rethinking what she had planned to do. She seemed like a woman on the verge of something, and I really didn't want to be on the other side of that verge.

"Whatever," she barked.

"Please grab your belongings, leave this kitchen, and the hotel," Nicole continued. "You're fired."

"Oh, perfect! This is just what we need right now." Peter threw up his hands.

"This is crap!" She pointed at Peter. "This is your fault. If you hadn't come here mouthing off at me..."

Steadily, Nicole said, "I'm giving you fifteen minutes to grab your stuff and vacate the premises, Colleen. Peter, you can leave, too."

"Or what?" Colleen took a step toward Nicole. "What are you going to do, you uppity cow?"

Oh no she didn't! "Don't say that to her," I snapped.

Peter grabbed her arm. "Let's go, Colleen. Don't make things worse."

She pulled out of his grasp, grabbed the closest thing to her arm, which just happened to be a big cast-iron frying pan, and rushed forward.

I pushed Nicole out of the way just as Colleen swung the heavy skillet. I felt the air on my face as it whiffed past me.

The momentum of the swing twisted Colleen's body slightly, so I was able to come in close, grab her wrist holding the pan, and crank her arm. She instantly dropped the heavy pan, and it landed with a heavy thud inches from my feet. She tried to punch me in the jaw, but she didn't make it. I ducked, grabbed her around the waist, and pulled her down to the floor onto her stomach. Not the smoothest or prettiest maneuver, but it worked. I sat on her back to keep her still while Nicole called the sheriff.

Chapter Fourteen

AFTER THE SHERIFF ARRIVED and contained the situation, which meant arresting Colleen and calming Nicole and the whole Park family, we were all carted down to the station so he could take statements and book Colleen for assault. It was all pretty surreal, to be honest. You'd think, after finding my second dead body, that giving witness statements would be old hat. It wasn't.

"So, what happened after Nicole fired Colleen and asked her to leave?"

"She got really angry, grabbed an iron skillet from the counter, and tried to hit Nicole with it."

"Do you think she intended to harm Nicole?"

I thought for a moment, making sure I'd read the situation right. "Yeah. I'm sure."

"Okay." He finished writing some notes in his report, then set the pen down and leaned back in his chair, eyeballing me. "I think maybe this is a record for crimes observed by one civilian witness on Frontenac Island in less than a month, Andi."

"Do I get a prize or something?"

Chuckling softly, he shook his head. "Nope. Nothing as cool as that."

"So, after what I told you about her argument with Peter, do you think it's likely Colleen pushed Mrs. Walker down the stairs?"

"It's certainly possible. She had motive and the means."

"What about opportunity?"

He paused a moment, as if he was making a decision. "Yeah, she had the opportunity. We found a witness who saw her at Mrs. Walker's house around the time of death."

I nodded and arched my eyebrows. "Are you going to charge her?"

"You can wipe that smirk off your face. Yes, I already knew about Colleen before you told me. The evidence is still circumstantial, but we've got enough to justify some warrants," he replied, cagey as ever.

So I gave him another little push. "Follow the money, right? They were broke and stand to inherit everything she had. I heard Mrs. Walker invested smartly."

"I'll look into it," he replied.

"Can I go now?"

He gestured toward the door. "You may."

I stood and turned to make my exit.

"Hey, Andi?"

I flipped back around to look at him.

"I don't condone all of your actions, but…good job saving Nicole from serious harm."

I grinned. This was a high compliment indeed, especially from the usually stoic Sheriff Jackson. "Thank you, Luke. That means a lot."

His eyebrows came up at my use of his first name, but I figured we were long past formalities, at least in private. I wouldn't dare call him that in public. People would assume things that weren't true if I did. Frontenac Island was nothing if not a hotbed of gossip.

I walked out of his office and into a flurry of activity in the lobby of the station. All the noise was coming from some people I knew well. Three Parks were heading right for me, talking over each other. Lois reached me first, actually nudging Ginny aside, and pulled me into a tight hug.

"Thank God you were there. I can't even imagine what would have happened if you hadn't been," she whispered in my ear. "Henry and I were so worried!"

When she released me, Ginny took her place, squeezing me so tight I could barely breathe. "You're like Wonder Woman. Protecting us from evildoers."

"I was just in the right place at the right time." Although I felt like I had somehow done more bad than good. Saving Nicole from harm was definitely good, but maybe Colleen wouldn't have snapped if I hadn't been there in the first place. A lot of her rage had been directed at me.

Eric was next to hug me, but he was a bit bumbling and awkward, probably due to the incident with Nicole that had preceded this whole thing. "Thank you."

"Where is Nicole?" I looked around the lobby, noticing her absence.

"She's with the deputy, making her statement," Eric said.

"Is she okay?"

"Yeah, she is. Just shook up a bit, but all in one piece because of you," Eric replied.

The most glaring absence was Samuel's. I wondered if he didn't know about the melee or had simply decided that golf with my rival, Casey, was more important. I hoped it was the former. I'd hate to think Casey was more important to him than his grandson's wife.

Ginny put her arm around me and said in a low voice, "Let's see Casey Cushing take down a skillet-wielding maniac." She giggled.

"Yeah, but a skillet-wielding maniac on the staff won't be good press for the hotel," I said. "Samuel won't like this at all."

Ginny puffed her chest. "But that's not your fault."

"True."

And it wasn't my fault, but that hadn't stopped Samuel from blaming anything on me before. Why would it matter now?

CHAPTER FIFTEEN

GINNY AND I WALKED out of the sheriff's station, and a microphone and camera were instantly thrust into my face. My eyes bugged out just as the local reporter, Tanya Walsh, asked her first question.

"Miss Steele, again you're involved in a violent altercation with a person connected to the Park Hotel. Care to comment?"

Ginny got in her face, backing her up a step or two. "Andi just saved my sister-in-law's life. She's a hero. The Park Hotel is proud to have her as concierge."

Tanya wasn't the least bit fazed by Ginny's defense of me. "Isn't it true, Ms. Steele, that you're under investigation for embezzlement?"

"What?" I blurted. "Where did you get that information?"

"I can't expose my sources."

"Your sources are full of—"

It was Mayor Lindsey Hamilton who cut me off. "I just heard about your heroics," she said to me. Then she smiled at

Tanya and into the camera, ever the consummate politician. "On behalf of the town, I'd like to commend you, Andi Steele, on your quick thinking and selfless defense of others." She shook my hand. I was acutely aware that my wrist flopped like a limp noodle.

"Thank you, Mayor," I said, gazing into the camera and trying to look...I don't know, Wonder Womanly.

We stood like that for a few more moments while a photographer took a slew of video. As my smile was plastered to my face, I looked past the camera and the reporter and saw Daniel Evans standing at the bottom of the steps, beaming up at me with his megawatt smile. My belly did a few somersaults. The man had a potency level of the god of thunder himself.

After Mayor Lindsey released me, I walked down the steps toward Daniel.

"Hey," I said.

"Hey yourself. It seems you're in the thick of things again."

"It's my superpower." I shrugged. "What are you doing in town?"

"I had a meeting with Lindsey to discuss some mayoral things."

"Secret mayoral things?"

"Are there any other kind?" He chuckled and waved toward a nearby golf cart. "I have to catch the ferry soon, but can I give you a lift back to the hotel?"

Ginny took that moment to join us. She smiled at Daniel, then looked at me, then looked at Daniel. "Never mind." She went up the steps to find Lois and Eric, who were still waiting for Nicole.

I nodded toward Daniel. "Sure, you can drive me. That would be nice."

He led me to the golf cart parked at town hall. It was silver and sleek and suited him. I slid onto the buttery-soft leather seat. When he got in, I was stroking my fingers over the seat.

"Nice ride."

"Yeah, I like it." He started the electric engine and pulled onto the street. I imagined it killed him to only be allowed to putter along on the island. I heard he drove a bright red BMW Roadster over on the mainland which was made to hug curves at high speeds.

"So, you haven't called me," he said.

I pressed my lips together, trying to play it cool, when my heart was thumping pretty hard and fast. "Yeah, I've been busy. Since Samuel Park's sudden return to the Park Hotel, he's been running me ragged. For some reason, he blames me for any and all bad press the hotel gets."

Daniel's face clouded. "I heard about what happened today. I'm sure he won't blame you for that."

"Oh, I'm sure he'll find a way."

Unfortunately, the ride up to the hotel only took ten minutes, and then Daniel was parking the cart. We both got out, and he walked with me into the hotel. Once in the lobby, I suddenly felt self-conscious.

"Thank you for the ride."

"I'll see you to your suite, if that's okay."

I nodded that it was indeed *very* okay.

As we walked, my palms actually started to sweat. I felt like I was a teenager again on my first date. This just proved how long it had been since my last date. Over a year, for sure. I was rusty at flirting, although I'd never been all that proficient at the dating game. Sometimes I just didn't see the signals, or I misread them. When it came to business, I was a shark. Personal life—a kitten.

"So, do you like being the mayor of Frontenac City?" I asked lamely.

"Yeah, I do. I like working in service of my town. I'm good at it."

"You're good at being humble, too," I grinned. Maybe I had more talent for this flirting thing than I'd thought.

He chuckled. "I think a person should be confident in what they do well. I'm sure you would agree."

"I do. I was a really, really good lawyer." I was surprised to hear the wistfulness in my voice.

"I believe you," he said. "I'd heard you had to leave it. Do you mind me asking why?"

I licked my lips nervously. I didn't want to scare him away. But if he couldn't handle the truth, he wasn't worth the time anyway. He'd find out sooner or later, and it might as well come here and now and from me. "My boss was embezzling from our clients. My firm suspended me to protect themselves because of how many cases I had worked on with him."

He winced. "Ouch. That must've hurt."

I cleared my throat. "It did. Does. More than I want to admit."

"How did you end up here? Not that 'here' is such a bad place." He smiled warmly, and I nearly melted.

"Ginny is my best friend. We went to college together. I've known the Parks for years. So when I told her what happened, she just said, 'Get your butt out here.' So I put my stuff in storage and hopped on a plane. Just me and my two cats."

"Ginny sounds like a brilliant friend."

"She is. I don't think we truly know who is supposed to be in our lives until trouble hits. That's when the wheat gets separated from the chaff, as my nanny used to say."

"Very true," he agreed, nodding. "How did you end up being the concierge of the hotel?"

"Serendipity. Casey, who *was* the concierge, had to take time off when his mother had surgery, so Ginny pushed Lois to hire me."

"I appreciate serendipity."

I met his gaze and smiled. "As do I."

We arrived at the door of my suite, and I suddenly wished that the corridor had been twice as long. "Thank you for walking me."

"Any time." He took a moment to really look into my eyes. His gaze also flitted over my mouth, and I had to suppress the urge to lick my lips. Then he took a tiny step back. "Remember, if you ever get to the mainland, call me, and we'll have lunch or dinner or whatever."

"Sounds good. And same for you when you're back in town."

He smiled. "I would call, but you never gave me your number."

"Oh. Crap. I'm sorry."

"No worries. You can make it up to me." He took out his phone and passed it over. I entered my name and number, then gave it back to him. He slid it into his pocket. "I will now bid you a good day." He tipped his head to me as he would have tipped a hat in a bygone era when the Park Hotel was new.

I watched him walk away for a moment and then blurted, "Did you send me flowers yesterday?"

"Ah, no, I did not."

"Okay, sorry. I was just wondering. I got this gorgeous bouquet with a note but no signature."

"Hmm, do I need to worry about competition?"

I blushed. "I don't know, do you?"

"Maybe it was Sheriff Jackson." He chuckled.

"Why is everyone saying that? Why on earth would the sheriff send me flowers? We don't even really get along."

"I was just joking. The man is the definition of stoic, and I can't imagine him sending flowers to anyone."

"Right?" I took out my keycard to my room. "Okay, I won't detain you any longer. Be gone with you. Back to the mainland."

He gave me a little salute and walked away down the corridor.

I went into my suite, dumped my keycard and purse on the little foyer table, then collapsed onto the sofa in the living room. After kicking off my shoes, I leaned my head back on the cushions and closed my eyes with a sigh. What a day. All I wanted to do now was to get some food and just sit here and read a book. If I didn't have to talk to anyone again until tomorrow morning, I would be a very happy woman.

A knock came at the door. Smiling, I went to open it. Maybe Daniel forgot to tell me something, or maybe he returned for a kiss. Could have been wishful thinking, but I had a sense that he had wanted to kiss me.

I threw open the door. "Did you forget something?"

Except it wasn't Daniel standing there.

Peter Walker shuffled from foot to foot as he looked down at me. "I need your help."

Chapter Sixteen

I WAS STARTLED TO see Peter shadowing my doorway. He wasn't a big man, but he was tall and had an imposing manner about him. He didn't seem like a pleasant sort at all. "I'm not sure what I can do for you, Peter."

"The word around the hotel is that you can help people out."

"Yeah, with small legal matters."

"That's not all, from what I've heard." He scrubbed at his chin, where dark whiskers were poking through. "Colleen did not kill my aunt. She's a lot of things, but a murderer is not one of them."

I wasn't persuaded. "She could've killed Nicole with that skillet today."

He sighed. "She's impulsive and reckless. But she's not a killer."

"She also has a temper. And lacks self-control," I added.

He screwed up his lips, tilted his head. "Okay. But I swear she didn't kill Aunt Ida. She didn't."

"How do you know for sure? She was at the house on the day your great-aunt died."

"I know—because I asked her to go. I was parked down the street waiting for her. She was in and out in ten minutes tops."

The neighbors, Blue and Sunglasses, never mentioned seeing Peter. But if he had parked down the street like he said, they wouldn't have. "Why was she at the house that day?"

He rubbed his face again, getting irritated. I had a sudden urge to slam the door shut in his face. What if his temper was as volatile as his wife's? Was I in danger?

I said, "Look, I think you should talk to a lawyer…"

"I thought you were one."

"I can't practice law here. Any advice I might give you wouldn't be reliable."

"Colleen went there to get something for me, okay?"

"What?"

"A couple of silver picture frames."

I frowned. The conversation I had with JC and Reggie replayed in my mind. They'd called Peter "Poor Peter" because he was always broke. He was in a lot of debt, and his great-aunt was as miserly as they come.

Understanding dawned. "You're pawning off her stuff. Because you need the money."

He nodded sheepishly. At least he suffered some guilt. "Do you know what it's like taking care of someone like that? So cheap, so selfish. She had oodles of money, and she knew Colleen and I were in a bad way. But not once did she ever offer to help us out. Not once."

His sense of entitlement was not surprising. Mrs. Walker might have helped him out from time to time. But she wasn't legally required to do so. And he had to know that. "I'm sorry to hear about your troubles, but I'm not sure what you think I can do."

"Talk to the sheriff. The word is he listens to you."

I nearly laughed. "Not sure where you heard that, but it's so not true."

The muscles along his jawline clenched. "We have nothing to gain from Aunt Ida's death. She was worth more to us alive than dead. There was always the chance that she'd help us out. Now, she never will. Why would we kill her?"

I was going to bring up his aunt's rumored wealth and the house. Being her next of kin, he'd normally inherit that. But maybe I was missing something. Maybe there was a will with alternative bequests.

Before I could ask, my cell phone buzzed from its perch on the foyer table. "Excuse me for a minute." I snagged the phone and answered.

"Andi? It's Shannon from Blossom. I have those dresses you wanted."

"Right. Excellent. Can you have them delivered to the hotel?"

"I sure can."

I turned back to the door to tell Peter I'd be just another minute, but he was gone. I poked my head out the door but didn't see him anywhere. Warily, I closed the door and locked it.

"Thanks, Shannon. The bride will be ecstatic."

After hanging up with her, I took out the piece of paper with the bride-to-be's number on it and called her. She answered right away.

"Hi, Melanie. It's Andi Steele, concierge for the Park Hotel. We talked about your, uh, wedding plans."

"Hey, Andi." Both words were slightly drawn out, like "Heyyy AAndiee," which gave me a slight suspicion that she'd been drinking.

"I got your dresses."

"Yay!" There was some cheering in the background. She must've been celebrating with her bridesmaids already.

"When the dresses arrive at the hotel, I'll have them delivered to your room."

"Can you bring them yourself?"

"You want *me* to bring them?"

"Yes, then you can help us celebrate. Woo-hoo!" There were several parroted "woo-hoos" in the background.

I sighed. This was not going to end well. "Yes, of course. I'll deliver them myself."

"Thanks, Andi." She disconnected.

I was still unsure about this whole wedding with Melanie and Karl. It was clearly a mistake, but it wasn't up to me to point that out. My job was to make sure everything was planned precisely the way the guest requested. It was not my place to make judgments. They weren't planning anything illegal or immoral, so basically I should provide the services Melanie asked for and keep my opinions to myself.

It was just that I knew Karl. And I knew without a shadow of a doubt, when he hit on Melanie at the bar last night, he had no plans then, or ever, to marry her tonight. I needed to find him to make sure he did the decent thing and confessed the truth. Soon.

Until he did, though, I had to make sure I didn't drop the ball. I didn't want to give Samuel more ammunition to fire me.

After I did a quick freshen-up in my suite, I headed to the restaurant to make sure Justin had the sandwiches and pastries ready for the wedding reception. It would also give me a chance to check up on Nicole, although I didn't imagine she'd be back in her office after what had happened earlier. She was probably safely tucked away at home with her family around her.

As I walked through the restaurant toward the kitchen, I thought about Peter's visit. I should tell the sheriff about it, for sure. I couldn't keep information like that to myself. If Colleen was innocent of murdering her husband's great-aunt, I certainly didn't want her to go through an unnecessary rigorous investigation. She was already charged with assault. She didn't need a murder charge on her head as well.

I caught up with Chef Justin just as he was leaving.

"Everything ready for the Lawson wedding?"

He nodded. "Yup, everything's prepared and chilling in the cold room. It's all labeled."

"Good. Thanks."

"I heard what happened earlier. Are you all right?"

"Oh yeah, I'm fine. I don't think she was aiming at me."

"But she could've hit you, from what I heard. You saved Nicole."

I shrugged. "Anyone would've reacted the same."

He gave me a look. "I don't know about that. I think a lot of people would've just tried to save their own ass." He patted me on the shoulder, then left the restaurant for the evening.

I checked on the food for the wedding—it was indeed labeled so well that anyone could understand it—then went back to the lobby. The dresses had arrived.

Holly waited to handle alterations. I ushered her into the concierge closet, which was a huge room where porters could leave luggage and other deliveries for guests.

Inside, on a rolling hanger, were four gorgeous dresses. The bride's dress was an off-white lace-and-ruffle number. It was very Victorian, and even had a fan and umbrella to match. The bridesmaid dresses were simple V-necked shifts—one was lilac, another sea-foam green, and the other a very subtle peach. All elegant.

I smiled at Holly. "Ready for battle?"

She laughed. "Oh yes, believe me, I've dealt with last-minute wedding alterations before."

"Good. Because this is my first time." I called a porter and said, "Follow me."

A few minutes later, I knocked on the door to Melanie's hotel suite. It opened, and one of her bridesmaids, Sheila, pulled Holly and me in with a very wobbly smile. They had definitely been drinking. There were several empty wine bottles littered around the room. The bride-to-be was sprawled out on the sofa, one fuzzy slipper on, the other dangling from her big toe.

I was pretty sure it was time for an intervention.

As the other girls fawned and squealed over the dresses, I whispered to Holly to not make any alternations to them yet. I stood over Melanie.

She smiled up at me. "AaaAndiee."

"I'm wondering if you've heard from Karl."

She pouted. "No. I've texted him a bajillion times."

"Then maybe it's not such a good idea to plan a wedding," I said kindly. "The groom should be involved."

"But he said he loved meeeeee."

"I'm sure he did, Melanie. You're a loveable girl."

"I am?" She grabbed my hand and tried to pull me down to her. I stood my ground.

"Do your parents know about the wedding?"

She frowned. "No. But they wouldn't understand. They don't believe in love at first sight."

"Don't you want your parents to be at your wedding? It's such a huge step to take without the support and love of family."

She slapped her hands over her face and started to sob. She was saying words, but they were muffled, and I couldn't make out anything.

All three of her friends piled on top of her to soothe her. Sheila glared at me. "What did you say to her?"

"Probably things maybe you three should've been telling her."

"You're not very nice," one of the other girls said.

"I know. I'm a horrible person," Sheila replied.

I glanced over at Holly, who was looking uncomfortable and wringing her hands near the dress rack. I went over to her. "I'm going to go out on a limb here and say there won't be dress fittings today."

The porter asked, "Do you want me to take the dresses back to the concierge closet?"

"Yeah. We'll keep them there until I know for sure that they can go back to Blossom. Thanks for the indulgence."

Holly smiled and patted me on the arm. "No problem. Good luck with…" She gestured to the gaggle of girls on the sofa.

"Thanks."

Holly opened the suite door, and the porter rolled the rack out.

Melanie popped up from the sofa, mascara streaks like stripes down her flushed cheeks. "Where are the dresses going?"

"Just downstairs to my special storage."

"But aren't we going to try them on?" Sheila whined.

I ignored her and eyed Melanie. "I think you know the right thing here."

She crossed her arms over her chest. "I want to talk to Karl."

"I want to talk to him, too, actually." I shook my head. "I have tried to track him down. He's not at his apartment or at any of his usual hangouts."

"I'm not canceling anything until I talk to him."

"Okay, I'll find him and bring him here to talk to you. Until we get back, why don't you take a nap?" I turned to the drunken bridesmaids. "In fact, all of you should take a nap. So you'll be ready for the big event tonight."

Instead of thanking me, Melanie picked up a near-empty bottle of wine on the side table and tipped it back to her mouth. She collapsed on the sofa again, and her girls surrounded her like bubble wrap encasing something fragile. I appreciated their friendship wall of support. Melanie would need it, regardless of how all of this turned out.

I left her suite and went down to the lobby. As I marched across the floral carpet to the front doors, I saw Ginny.

"You look like a woman on a mission," she said.

"I am. Want to help me hunt for Karl?"

"Oh hell yeah." She pumped her fist into the air, then frowned. "But we need snacks for this mission." She jogged over to the Lady Slipper Tea Room and grabbed a couple of bottles of Kombucha and some rice chips.

Now that we had supplies, we walked out of the hotel and commandeered a cart. We were on hotel business, and there was no way I was going to walk around the village for hours on end looking for Karl. There wasn't much daylight left, and I needed to find him before seven o'clock—to keep Melanie from being left at the altar.

CHAPTER SEVENTEEN

GINNY AND I DROVE around the main village for an hour, popping into every drinking establishment we came across, looking for Karl. We stopped by the historical society office again—the "ten-minute" sign was still on the door—and checked his apartment. Nothing. No sign of him. I thought briefly about visiting his sister, Dr. Neumann, at the hospital, but thought again—that might be bad form.

As we pulled away from the curb behind the historical society building and rolled out onto Main Street, my gaze swept over the ferry dock and where JC and Reggie always sat playing their game of chess.

"Stop the cart!"

Ginny jerked us to a stop in the middle of the road. A horse-drawn taxi honked its horn and came to a noisy halt behind us. "What?"

I pointed toward the dock. "There's Karl."

She pulled the cart over to the curb near the Swan Song bar, and we jumped out and hurried down the dock toward the ferry station. Karl seemed engaged in a lively conversation with Reggie and JC, based on his hands gesturing this way and that. When we approached and he noticed us, his hands dropped to his side, and he visibly sagged.

He knew why we were there.

"Hello, Karl," I said evenly.

He held his hands up in front of him, palms out. "I know what you're going to say."

"Is that so?" I lifted an eyebrow at him.

He pouted like a schoolboy being scolded. "I should never have led Melanie on."

"No, you shouldn't have. And you're an ass for doing so. But you are an even bigger ass for not calling her back and telling her the truth. That poor girl ordered a wedding cake, reception food, a wedding dress."

Reggie got to his feet and smacked Karl in the back of the head. "What the hell did you do, boy?"

"He let this poor girl that he just met think he was going to marry her. Tonight."

Reggie smacked him again before Karl could dodge out of the way.

Karl said, "I know. It's just…we drank so much, and she is very persuasive."

Ginny crossed her arms and tapped her foot. "Tell me you are *not* going to put this whole debacle on her."

He put his hand up to ward off Ginny's anger. "I know. I know."

"You have a chance to make it right," I said.

"How?"

"Come with us to the hotel and talk to Melanie. Let her down easy. Tell her how beautiful and desirable she is, but you can't get married."

"I don't want to break her heart," he said, and I believed he actually meant it. Karl wasn't a callous man. He was just a reckless one, especially when it came to women.

Ginny still tapped her foot. I waited. Reggie and JC seemed like they might give Karl a couple more whacks for good measure.

Karl looked at all of us, ran his hands through his long, dark hair, and sighed heavily. "Okay."

We all piled into the golf cart and went back up the hill. When we reached the hotel, I thought I was going to have to literally pull Karl across the lobby, he was dragging his feet so much. I turned and gave him an admonishing look, and he thankfully picked up the pace. Ginny had been distracted by a call from Clinton, and her smile was so huge as she talked, I didn't have the heart to force her to accompany us to Karl's impending slaughter. Although Karl was no lamb. He was more like a fox. Quick to play, and quicker to hide if given the chance. Which I would not do.

CHAPTER EIGHTEEN

STANDING IN FRONT OF the door to Melanie's suite, I had to grab Karl's wrist before he bolted. I'd never seen someone sweat so much in my life. Strands of his silky hair were stuck to his forehead, and he had sweat stains down the sides of his shirt.

I knocked twice, and the door opened.

I ushered Karl into the lionesses' den. Four sets of eyeliner-rimmed cat eyes glared at him. I felt a little bad for him. He'd made a big mistake, and he was definitely paying for it.

Melanie jumped up from the sofa where I'd left her. "I've been calling you."

"I know." He gnawed on his bottom lip, trying to keep his gaze on Melanie and not the three other women throwing eye daggers at him.

"Okay, c'mon ladies. Let's leave these two to talk." I gestured toward the door.

"Where are we supposed to go?" Sheila asked.

"Drinks are on me down in the lounge," I said.

The girls high-fived before quickly leaving the room. I glanced at Melanie to make sure she would be okay without her posse. She had her hands on her hips and was just about to launch into a full-on rant, so I figured she had the situation handled.

I followed the young women down to the lounge and informed the bartender, Rodney, that their drinks were on the house. After much persuasion, I sat at the bar and joined them for one drink.

As they chatted about everything from "how much alcohol was really in their drinks" to one of the girl's embarrassing tan lines, I halfheartedly listened, laughing politely when called for a response. These young women were a good ten years younger than I was…and so much was different for them. Social media was a huge influencer for them, and all of that nonsense was barely a blip on my radar.

When the conversation turned to college and their excitement and dread of returning to it for their senior years in the fall, I thought about when I'd first started at University of Michigan. I remembered moving my stuff into my dorm room, excited for the future, scared of being alone, and meeting Ginny. She'd hugged me the first instant we'd met. From that moment, our friendship had been solidified.

I envied them their naïve enthusiasm for what was to come. I was like that all through the years at U of M, and only slightly less so at Stanford Law School afterward. Even my first years working at Alcott, Chambers & Rucker were full of anticipation.

It had been six years later, there at that very firm, when Derek Alcott told me that my boss, Jeremy, had embezzled millions—that's when my naivety had vanished in an instant. I still had hopes, though, of practicing law again. Not at that firm.

I wouldn't go back to those snakes on a bet. But somewhere else. I was a lawyer in my heart. Not a concierge. All this stuff I'd had to deal with in the past few days was proof positive that being a concierge was not my highest and best calling, for sure. Maybe I should've admitted defeat and saved Samuel the time and energy necessary to get rid of me. Get out of Casey's way and move on. Somewhere that would let my cats come back home, too.

"Hold up, girls." Sheila held up her cell phone. "Melanie says everything's good."

"What does that mean? Are they still getting married?" the blond girl, Becky, asked as she literally licked the inside of her mojito glass, trying to get the last drop of alcohol.

"Wedding's off." Sheila read off the texts that were zipping through. "But the party is still on."

All the girls let out a "whoop-whoop" then got to their feet. As one entity, they moved out of the lounge. Sheila waved at me. "Thanks, Andi. You saved our girl."

"You're welcome. Keep each other safe, okay?"

"We will."

I got up and followed them out.

Then I heard Becky say, "We should call that Todd guy and get some weed."

"What guy?" the third girl—couldn't remember her name—asked.

"You know the cute guy with the spiky black hair."

"Oh, him. Yeah, he was cute."

Before Becky could run off, I touched her shoulder, and she turned around. "This Todd person…does he work at the D&W?"

She shrugged. "I don't know. We met him the other night outside the Swan. Him and his girl. Hannah, I think, was her name. She was selling some cheap jewelry."

"What kind of jewelry?"

"I don't know…cheap gold and silver stuff. Earrings and some necklaces."

I nodded. "Okay, thanks."

"You're not going to narc on us, are you?"

"No. But be careful, okay? You're all adults, but I kind of feel responsible for you now." I chuckled.

"We'll be careful, I promise." She gave me a big grin, then caught up with the rest of the girls as they piled into the elevator.

My cell phone buzzed with a text message. It was from Melanie.

Thank you, and had a smiley face and a heart beside it.

I smiled as I slid my phone into my purse. My work here was finished. I called Blossom and told them to come pick up the dresses from the concierge closet. I then went into the restaurant kitchen and tracked down the servers getting ready for the wedding reception. The food was already laid out on carts.

"So," I said, "the event has been canceled."

One of the servers shook her head. "What do we do with the sandwiches and desserts?"

"Well, it has all been paid for." I plucked a scrumptious-looking pastry from the tray and plopped it into my mouth. When I was done chewing, I said, "Anyone hungry? I know I am."

CHAPTER NINETEEN

IN MY SUITE, I folded myself onto the sofa, a plate of pastries and finger sandwiches at the ready. I picked up my notebook and pen from the table and started to doodle. This exercise quickly turned into a list. Lists always made me happy and calmed my mind.

This was what I knew about Mrs. Walker's death.

1. She died between the hours of 10 a.m. and noon.
2. Fell (pushed?) down the stairs, probably broke her neck
3. Colleen Walker visited the house around 11 a.m.
4. Todd from D&W delivered groceries to her house
5. Her dog Lulu went missing a week before
6. Next door neighbor Mr. Rainer took her dog
7. Mr. Rainer and Mrs. Walker had several altercations over the years
8. Mrs. Walker was not well liked around her neighborhood
9. Peter and Colleen Walker are in a lot of debt
10. They aim to inherit everything???? Maybe not????

I stopped to study my list and think about what wasn't on it.

Sheriff Jackson had told me Mr. Rainer had an alibi. But what if his cleaning woman lied? I mean, I had seen inside his house, and it didn't look like it had been properly cleaned in months.

Colleen was at Mrs. Walker's house, but Peter said she was in and out in ten minutes. Enough time to steal a few trinkets to pawn. Still plenty of time to shove someone down the stairs.

Todd the delivery boy had told the sheriff he was rushed, couldn't put away Mrs. Walker's groceries that day. Why was he rushed? If he had done something to Mrs. Walker, though, Colleen would have seen it because she was there after him. But what's to say he actually was there earlier? We only had his word for it. Maybe he actually came after Colleen.

I didn't know for sure, but there was something up with this Todd dude. When I'd seen him at the store, he'd acted like something was wrong. He could've had a lover's spat with his girlfriend Hannah, but maybe it was more. According to the college girls, Todd was selling weed near the docks. And Hannah was selling cheap jewelry. Maybe Colleen hadn't been the only one stealing stuff from cranky Mrs. Walker. Maybe Todd had stolen trinkets from her when he delivered the groceries, too.

I had to talk to the sheriff. Let him know that Peter had come to me. I couldn't keep that to myself. I also wanted to find out about Mrs. Walker's will. If Peter and Colleen were set to inherit everything, that could prove to be a substantial motive. But then why steal stuff from her? Stuff they would eventually own, probably. But if they weren't set to inherit, then killing her would eliminate their golden goose. Peter was right about that.

I knew I shouldn't even be worrying about these things. But I was kidding myself. I became involved the moment I stepped into that house. There was a lot of responsibility that went along with finding a dead person. And I wasn't one for shirking responsibility.

I crawled into bed with my list, thinking I'd scribble a few more notes if anything came to me before I nodded off. But I added nothing more…because I fell asleep in a snap, pen still in hand.

CHAPTER TWENTY

THANKFULLY, I'D ENJOYED A decent sleep last night and was heavily caffeinated when all hell broke loose in the hotel lobby.

I was feeling on top of my game when Melanie's parents stormed into the hotel, swirling across the lobby like two dervishes and up to their daughter's suite. The porters and front receptionists were in a tizzy because the Lawsons were frequent, valued guests.

Shortly afterward, Lois and Samuel popped into the lobby to make sure everything was all right—but they'd missed the first wave of the dust storm, and all they could do was wait for it to circle back. They were both worried. I could tell because they snapped at everyone, not only me.

A half hour later, the Lawsons returned to the lobby with Melanie and her friends in tow. All the girls had their heads down, dragging their Jimmy Choos, gnawing on their glossed-up lips. They all marched toward the concierge desk as one unstoppable locomotive, and I thought I was going to have a heart attack right there and then when I saw the hard looks on Mr. and Mrs. Lawson's faces.

Oh God, here it comes. This is how it all ends.

"Andi Steele?" Mr. Lawson asked.

"Yes, that's correct, Mr. Lawson. How may I help you?"

Out of the corner of my eye, I saw Samuel lurking nearby, likely gleefully anticipating my demise. He was probably the one who called Mr. Lawson with the disturbing news about his daughter's behavior. It would be exactly like Samuel to do something like that.

Lois sidled up to the desk. She shook hands with the Lawsons, one at a time. "Nice to see you again, Michael. Lavinia. Will you be staying the night?"

"No, we just came to collect our daughter," Michael Lawson said. He glanced over at Melanie, who had been thoroughly admonished. She wouldn't even lift her head.

Lois, bless her, persisted. "Is there anything I can personally help you with?"

"I need to speak with Ms. Steele." He turned and glared at me.

Lois's eyes widened, and it looked like she wanted to play defense and block him from assaulting me. I appreciated the sentiment, even if sentiment was as far as her effort went. Samuel made no effort to interfere. He stood aside as if he were watching a theater production and waiting to pass judgment on our performances. Which he probably was.

I faced Mr. Lawson with confidence…well, bravado, actually. "How can I help?"

"I wanted to thank you for taking care of this situation. Melanie told us everything you've done for her."

I glanced at Melanie, who lifted her head and gave me a small, tight smile.

Relief flooded through me, and my legs felt like spaghetti. I grasped the desk to keep myself upright. I cleared my throat. "It was my pleasure, sir."

Mrs. Lawson joined her husband and grabbed my hand on the counter. "You have no idea the scandal you've thwarted, Ms. Steele. That girl just about made the biggest mistake of her life."

"We were all that young once, I think." I glanced toward Lois, unsure really of what to say in this situation.

"Maybe, but we would never have eloped with some disreputable lothario," Lavinia Lawson said. "What was she thinking?"

I gently pulled my hand out from under hers, careful not to insult. "Oh, Karl's not a bad guy. Just impetuous and reckless, much like Melanie, I assume."

"Yes, well…"

Mr. Lawson patted his wife's arm. "Regardless, we are in your debt, Ms. Steele."

"You're certainly welcome. I'm glad I could help."

He turned to Lois. "As always, the service at the Park Hotel is impeccable, Lois. You can absolutely rely on the Lawsons to recommend this place to everyone."

Lois's hand fluttered to her neck, and she actually blushed. "Thank you, Michael. Your business is always welcome and appreciated. Henry always enjoyed having you with us."

"We miss Henry, too," he said and paused to pat Lois's hand. Then he took out a white envelope from inside his suit jacket pocket and slid it across the desk to me. "This is for you. A small token. Thank you again."

I smiled at him and took the envelope. I didn't open it right there and then—that would've been rude—but from the feel of it, I'd say there was a very nice tip inside. "Have a safe trip home, and we hope to see you again soon."

"You will." He gave me a curt nod, then with his wife beside him and his daughter and her entourage trailing behind, they crossed the lobby to the front doors to catch the hotel's horse-drawn carriage to the island's private airport.

As Melanie passed the desk, she mouthed a silent thank-you to me.

I tilted my head and smiled, all motherly-like, feeling quite pleased with the turn of events. Truth be told, I was also a little bit sad that my parents couldn't sweep into my life any time they felt like it and interfere. Then again, I'd be really ticked off if they tried. The mere thought of Drew and Emily behaving like the Lawsons made me grin.

When they were gone, Lois gave me a quick hug under Samuel's still watchful eye. "Well done, Andi." Then she was off to who knew where. Lois was always rushing around. I could never keep track of her movements. Which was one of the reasons she was so often frightening. She popped up when I least expected her.

Samuel then approached my desk, his expression typical of his behavior toward me—grumpy. Still, I looked at him expectantly, hoping to relish the crow he was eating. Instead, he slapped a thick manila envelope down on the desk. "I need you to take these to town hall. They're the licenses and permits we need filed for the Flower Festival."

I was thoroughly disappointed. No joy for me. He expressed not one iota of appreciation, in his body language or anything else. Just gave me another errand to run.

What a jerk.

With that, I realized I might never win Samuel's approval. I had to accept that and move on and just hope he wasn't planning to move me right out the door. I hadn't even worked long enough to collect unemployment benefits if he fired me.

"Do these documents need to go to anyone in particular?" I asked, resigned in my servitude.

"Give them to Dolores. She's expecting you. And get going. You're already late." He then walked away, humming a little tune, all pleased with himself.

CHAPTER TWENTY-ONE

AFTER ASKING LANE TO watch the concierge desk—he was happy to do it—I decided to walk down to the village instead of taking one of the carts. I welcomed the fresh air and the walk. I'd been negligent on keeping up any type of exercise regimen. Despite not really eating *that* much, I was noticing some of my pants were feeling a bit snug—the effects of consuming all the amazing desserts around instead of some low-cal meals.

"Oh well, sue me," I said to no one in particular. And then I laughed at my own words.

Once I was on Market Street, I decided I would stop in at Daisy's and visit Scout and Jem, and of course, Mrs. Walker's dog, Lulu, on the way back to the hotel. I wanted to know what was going on with all of that. I still felt bummed out for causing the dog to be taken from Mr. Rainer. He had seemed very distraught to lose her. Maybe he and Lulu were good for each other. She'd certainly seemed happy and healthy enough. Who knew?

As I walked, I resisted the urge to pop into a few of the shops. Blossom had a really cute top displayed in the window. I stopped to just peek at it. No harm in peeking. Holly the seamstress opened the door and stuck her head out.

"Hey, Andi."

"Hey. Did you get the dresses back in good shape?"

"We did." She shook her head, then snickered. "That was some kind of something."

"Yeah. At least it worked out in the end." And it had. The Lawsons were saved from a disastrous set of nuptials, and I was five hundred dollars richer. Hence, the quick peek at the cute top. I could treat myself for another disaster diverted.

Holly's eyes narrowed knowingly. "That top would look killer on you."

"Yes, it would."

"Want me to ring it up for you?"

"Would you?" I said. "I have to go to the registry office, but I'll be back this way in about an hour."

"No problem." She ducked into the shop and stepped into the window display to grab the top for me.

I waved at her and continued on my way.

The town hall was a red-brick cube structure built in the 1940s. It housed the town council's meeting room, the mayor's office, registry office, and a couple of other municipal-type services. Next door was the sheriff's office, and behind that, the fire department. All very neat and tidy.

The main lobby was tall and wide, very welcoming even if a bit stark. As I walked down the corridor toward the registry office, I checked out the pictures on the walls. Past mayors and town council members. Past sheriffs and fire chiefs. I stopped at a picture of Sheriff Jackson. Not Luke, but his dad, Norman. So, being lawmen ran in the family. It didn't surprise me. The sheriff had that way about him. A way that had obviously been ingrained in him from childhood.

I continued walking until I reached the registry office. The door was propped open by a lime-green wedge with a little owl on it, and I went in. It was empty save for a plump, pleasant-looking woman sitting behind the counter. She was furiously typing on a computer keyboard.

When I approached the desk, she stopped typing and smiled. She pushed her coke-bottle glasses into her mass of dyed-blond curls. "Hello, dear. How may I help?"

"I'm Andi Steele from the Park Hotel. I'm looking for Dolores."

"You found her." She giggled, and it made her entire body jiggle.

I set the envelope down on the counter. "From Samuel Park."

She took it, opened it, and slid all the papers out. She quickly flipped through them. "How is Sam?"

"He's fine."

She smiled at me again, her eyes crinkling. "That's good to hear." Her cheeks pinkened a little.

Hmm. Is there a crush happening here?

"Everything looks in order. But I would expect nothing less."

"Anything I need to take back with me?"

"Oh no, dear, it's all good."

"Excellent. Well, have a great day."

"You, too."

I left the office and wandered down the hall. It wasn't until I was almost at the end when I realized I had made a right instead of a left from the registry. Sighing, I turned around to head back but stopped when I saw an open door with the words *Don Hobbs, Lawyer* on a tarnished nameplate.

He was the lawyer the guys at Frontenac Island Bubbles Soap Company had told me about. The horrible bigoted lawyer, according to them. He was also the only game in town and was likely handling the probate of Mrs. Walker's will.

I peered into the office, then knocked on the door and called out, "Mr. Hobbs?"

No answer.

I stepped inside and saw the cramped office was empty save for the mess on top of the old desk and the stack of books and magazines on the floor. I moved closer to the desk and spotted a cup of coffee, still steaming, and a half-eaten apple strudel, probably from the Weiss Strudel House.

Frowning, I also noticed the papers and folders on the floor beside the desk. I heard a distinctive groan. I came around the desk, only to see a man on the ground. Probably Mr. Hobbs. He was clutching his chest, blinking rapidly, his mouth working like a guppy fish.

"Mr. Hobbs?!" I crouched next to him.

He thumbed his chest and then gestured wildly with his other hand.

"You're having heart pain?" I slid my hand into my purse to grab my phone to call 9-1-1. He grabbed my arm and groaned again. "It'll be okay. Help will be on its way."

He slapped the phone from my hand and reached for his desk. He grunted again.

"Do you have pills?"

He nodded furiously.

I turned and pulled open his desk drawers, searching for a pill bottle. I found one in the second drawer. I showed it to him. "Is this it?"

He grabbed my arm again. I opened the top, fished out a pill, and put into his mouth. He swallowed it down, then collapsed back onto the floor. I grabbed my phone and made the call to emergency.

Mr. Hobbs seemed to be stabilizing. He wasn't clutching his chest any longer, and his breathing seemed to be evening out. I looked around, trying to find something to make him more comfortable, when my gaze landed on an open file folder. The papers had scattered everywhere, probably when he fell. I gathered them together and noticed that it was Mrs. Walker's will and preliminary probate papers.

Well, lookee here.

I did a cursory glance through. Mrs. Walker had left the bulk of her estate to the town and not to her great-nephew Peter. It appeared that she wanted her house and lot to be turned into a bird sanctuary of some sort. And a few other surprises I hadn't expected. Peter and Colleen were to inherit nothing from her. So, killing her wouldn't have been advantageous for them at all. Just as Peter had claimed.

"What are you doing?"

I looked up to see Sheriff Jackson filling the doorway.

I stood and placed the folder back on the desk. He came over to where I was and stared down at Mr. Hobbs collapsed on the floor at my feet, taking in greedy gulps of air. Then he glanced at me, his eyes narrowing suspiciously.

"I didn't give him a heart attack, I swear to God. The pastry probably did it."

Chapter Twenty-two

THE EMTS ARRIVED WITHIN five minutes and had picked up Mr. Hobbs and strapped him to a gurney. He had on an oxygen mask but still tried to talk to me. I gave him a smile and patted his hand. "You're welcome." Not sure if he was really trying to thank me, or if it was something else.

Once he was wheeled out, Sheriff Jackson turned his steely gaze onto me. "Okay. Explain. Now."

"Hey, I saved his life. Can't we just leave it at that?"

"No, we can't leave it at that."

I flinched. "No, of course not. Okay, I knocked on his door, came in, and found him on the floor behind his desk, struggling to breathe."

He looked around the room, then down at the desk. "You'd have to literally be standing right at his desk to have seen him on the floor, Andi."

I sighed. "I figured he would be handling Mrs. Walker's estate, so I came in to see if I could find out anything."

"And did you find out anything?"

I nodded. "It seems that Mrs. Walker left everything to the town. Peter and Colleen won't inherit."

"Uh-huh."

"Well, there goes motive, right? Why would Colleen kill her if they weren't going to benefit?"

"What makes you think they knew about the will? Maybe they thought they would inherit."

"Because Peter came to see me the other night and swears that Colleen didn't do it, that she was in and out of the house in ten minutes because he was waiting for her down the street. He might not have known about the will, but I'm not sure that's true."

He scowled. "And when were you going to tell me this?"

"Right now?"

"Why did Peter tell you all of this?"

I shrugged. "I guess he heard that I can help people who find themselves in over their heads."

"Did it ever occur to you that he approached you to intimidate you? You're the key witness in his wife's assault. You found his aunt's body."

"Yes, it occurred to me." I ran a hand up and down my arm, remembering the unease I'd felt with Peter looming over me in the threshold of my suite. We had been alone. There was no one around that could've helped me if I had needed it. But I hadn't needed any help. He'd left without a problem.

The sheriff was still talking. "That's not exactly the action of an innocent man."

I didn't respond, because he was right. I'd put myself into a dangerous situation. Again. Although to be fair, it wasn't like I'd invited Peter into my suite or anything. He'd shown up, uninvited. That wasn't my fault.

"Did you not learn anything at all the last time? The only reason I threw you a few bones was to make you stay out of this. Satisfy your ridiculously curious nature and allow you to move on to concierge things or whatever else you do in your spare time."

He was starting to piss me off. "In my defense, I *did* catch the right killer last time."

"Yeah, and got hurt in the process. Plus put other people in danger." He took his hat off and ran a hand through his hair. "Or did you forget about that part?"

"No, I didn't forget. It's still very much in my mind." I turned my head away from him, afraid my eyes were going to well up. I wasn't a crier, but his constant critical barrage on top of Samuel's constant badgering was starting to weigh on me.

He sighed. "Look, Andi. I know you're trying to do some good here. And despite all my reservations, you do sometimes have good instincts."

I glanced at him beneath my lashes, not quite ready to eyeball him straight on.

"But I can't have you running around thinking you're Magnum PI or something."

A smile formed on my lips. I couldn't resist. "You know that reference totally dates you. I was thinking more of the likes of Veronica Mars."

"Regardless of who you're trying to emulate—"

"I'm not trying to emulate anyone, Sheriff. I can't help it if people talk to me. I'm an approachable person. You'd think you would want to use that. It would help you. Not everyone trusts the police."

"Andi…"

I secured my purse over my shoulder and lifted my chin. "If you'll excuse me, Sheriff, I have errands to take care of." I marched toward the door.

"I don't want to see you get hurt. It would make me really…unhappy."

I stopped briefly but didn't turn around. I didn't know what to say to that, because I wasn't sure exactly what it meant. So, I just kept walking and left Mr. Hobbs's office.

CHAPTER TWENTY-THREE

I PICKED UP MY blouse from Blossom, as promised, then made my way to Daisy's kennels. I found her helping one of her groomers handle a particularly rambunctious shih-tzu getting a summer buzz cut. Little Lulu was happily barking at her side.

When Daisy saw me, she gave me a wave. Not wanting to disturb her, I headed toward the back to see my babies in their "suite." Scout and Jem immediately ran up to me, greeting me with enthusiasm, trilling and wrapping around my ankles. I missed them so much. I sat on the floor so I could hug them and play with them with equal zeal.

The second I sat down, they crawled on top of me. I pulled them close and put my face into their fur, inhaling their kitty scents, which was always very calming to me. They both responded with lots of purring and butting their heads against my face. They always knew when I needed their affection.

"I miss you guys."

Scout meowed in answer, and Jem just purred louder.

"Things aren't too good without you." Pet, pet, pet. Purr, purr, purr. "I'm lonely most of the time, and Samuel is running me ragged. Like, how much more do I have to do to prove myself? It's so frustrating."

I scratched both of them in the places they liked and dangled some feathery birds on sticks so they could chase them. My anxiety of the past few days faded away as I played with them. I didn't realize how much their presence calmed me until now because I'd never lived without them before. I couldn't go on much longer without having them back permanently in my home. I had to move out of the hotel. But before I did that, I had to make damn sure that my job was secure.

After I gave Scout and Jem goodbye kisses, I found Daisy at her desk. Lulu was on one of the nearby chairs, curled up into a ball and sleeping. Daisy smiled as I plopped down in one of the empty chairs and sighed.

"Tough day?" she asked.

"You wouldn't even believe it if I told you."

She laughed.

"How's your day going? How's Lulu?"

"She's settling in. Mr. Rainer has called me no less than ten times to check up on her."

"Really?"

"Yup, he calls and asks how much she's eating, how often has she gone piddle, is she playing with the other dogs...." She sighed loudly. "He sounds like a worried parent."

"Maybe we were wrong about him. Maybe he's not a horrible monster."

"Maybe not. I'm starting to think that Mrs. Walker may have been the monster. I knew a lot of people didn't like her, but I always thought that was just, you know, neighborhood rivalry."

I nodded. "It's hard to find out bad stuff about someone you knew and liked."

"I take it you have experience in that."

"Oh yeah. My old boss, Jeremy. I thought I knew him. But what I didn't know about him could probably fill a football stadium."

"That sucks," she said.

"It certainly does." Lulu perked up and looked at me. I reached over and patted her little head. She was definitely a cute dog. "Oh, hey, how did your meeting with the landlord go?"

"Okay, I think. He didn't seem too pleased with the changes I asked for."

"You're within your right to ask for them, Daisy, remember that."

"I will."

Speaking of landlords... "Hey, do you know of any good houses for rent in the village?"

"You thinking of moving out of the hotel?"

"Yeah, I need my cats. It's hard not being with them every day."

"I hear that. I don't know what I would do if I didn't live in the apartment above."

Before I could say anything else about it, the front door swung open and Mr. Rainer rushed in. The small amount of hair he had was shooting out all over his head, and his shirt was untucked and looked unwashed. He had gray bristles on his face. It looked like he hadn't shaved or washed in days.

"Mr. Rainer," Daisy said, getting to her feet.

"You!" He jabbed a finger at me. "You're the reason I lost her. You took her from me."

My hand fluttered at my throat. He'd pointed out the very thing I'd been worrying over. "That's not necessarily true."

He moved forward quicker than I thought he could possibly move and swept up Lulu into his arms. I stepped in his way to block him from leaving.

"I'm taking my dog," he said.

"Mr. Rainer, I don't think that's a good idea," I said.

"She needs me." Lulu licked his chin.

"It's obvious the dog loves you, but this is a complicated case. We have to operate by the rules and laws," Daisy said as she came around the desk to stand beside me. "I can't release her to you. I have to wait until I hear from Mrs. Walker's lawyer."

"But what if…what if that horrible man, Peter, takes her? He won't love her like I do."

"I'm sorry," Daisy said, "but I have to do what the law says." She slowly reached for Lulu. Mr. Rainer put up no fight as she gently took the dog from him and settled her into the crook of her arm. She hesitated briefly, then turned and walked to her desk.

Mr. Rainer slapped his hands over his face and started to sob. His whole body shook with the force of his emotion. I got a lump in my throat watching him. It was tough seeing him so broken.

I put my arm around his shoulders and led him to a chair. He sat, and I sat beside him. I reached for the Kleenex box nearby and handed a few tissues to him. He took them and wiped at his eyes.

"I'm sorry," I said.

He looked at me, still wiping his eyes. "I'm lost without Lulu. I don't know what I'll do if I don't get her back."

I glanced over at Daisy to make sure she was out of earshot. She was. She was busy talking to Lulu in a soothing tone.

"I'm going to tell you something, Mr. Rainer," I said in a low voice, "but you have to promise me you'll never tell anyone that I told you this."

He nodded. "Okay."

"Mrs. Walker left her estate to the town. Her house and her money. Nothing is going to Peter. And that includes Lulu."

His eyes widened, and he suddenly gripped my hand. He squeezed it hard. I winced at the power of his grip. "How do you know?"

"I saw her will. She actually left the care of Lulu to you."

"What? I don't understand."

"She named you in her will to take possession of Lulu."

"Why would she do that? We hated each other. We always fought over that dog."

"Maybe she knew how much you actually liked the dog. Maybe she knew you'd take good care of her."

He sagged into the chair as if the relief of the whole thing was too much to bear. I snagged him some more tissues, and he blew his nose, hard, making a harsh, honking sound.

He sniffled. "So, when can I have her back?"

I glanced over to make sure Daisy was still unaware of what we were discussing. But she was gone, probably to put Lulu in one of the dog rooms. "I'd say no more than another week. I imagine the will reading will be in the next few days. After Mr. Hobbs recuperates."

"What happened to Mr. Hobbs?"

"Oh, nothing. I'm sure he's fine now."

Once Daisy returned, she came over to us. She looked from me to Mr. Rainer. "Everything okay over here?"

"Everything's good. Mr. Rainer was just leaving, and he won't bother you again. Right, Mr. Rainer?"

He stood and nodded dumbly. "Right."

"So, I don't need to call the sheriff?" Daisy asked.

"No!" We barked at the same time.

Daisy's eyes narrowed, but she didn't say anything as Mr. Rainer brushed past her and left the kennels. Then her gaze trained on me.

"What was that about? How did you get him to leave?"

"I just reasoned with him, that's all."

"The words *reason* and *Mr. Rainer* just don't seem like they should go in the same sentence." She snickered.

I shrugged. "He must've had an epiphany. Sometimes that can happen to a man."

She looked at me like she didn't believe a single word I said. Smart girl.

Chapter Twenty-four

WHEN I RETURNED TO the hotel, all I could think about was grabbing a wrap from the tea shop and sitting down to eat it in relative peace and quiet, maybe outside on one of the benches in the gardens, maybe near the hedge cut to look like a swan. I hadn't eaten since the meager banana and croissant I had for breakfast in my suite. But, Samuel, naturally, had other plans for me.

He caught me just as I was crossing the lobby with my wrap and drink in a paper bag. "I need you to go into Frontenac City to deliver some contracts to a few companies for the Flower Festival."

"Right now?"

"No, not right now." He frowned.

Relief surged through me for a moment.

"You can eat your lunch first, but then, yes, you need to catch the ferry over before three o'clock."

And the relief dissipated as quickly as it came.

He handed me another thick manila envelope and a list of business addresses that I needed to visit. I took the envelope and just stared at him. He patted my shoulder—it always felt like such a condescending gesture—and marched away, back to wherever he liked to lurk to hatch new ways to torment me.

How the heck was I expected to find these places? I'd never been to Frontenac City. I didn't know where I was going. I took out my phone and called Ginny.

"Are you busy today?"

"Yeah, I have two clients coming in to talk about events. A wedding and a doctors convention. Why?"

"Because Samuel's asked me to go into Frontenac City to deliver some contracts. I don't know where I'm going. I've never been there."

"Ohhh, sorry. Wish I could help you out. Who else could you call? Who else knows the mainland? How about Nicole? She likes you now, since you saved her life."

"Not sure we are at best-friends level quite yet."

But I *did* know someone who knew Frontenac City well.

I hung up with her and then called Daniel.

He answered on the third ring. "Daniel Evans."

"Hey, it's Andi Steele. Ah, from the Park Hotel?"

He chuckled. "You know you don't have to explain where you're from. You could just say, 'Hey, it's Andi.' I promise I'll know who you are."

"Well, what if you have several Andis in your life?"

"I don't. Only one. Only you."

My belly did a little flip-flop at that, and my face went warm. Thank God he couldn't see it.

"That's, uh, good to know."

"Are you in town?"

"I will be, and that's why I called. I have a few businesses I need to visit for the hotel, and I have no idea where I'm going. So, I was wondering…"

"If I could be your tour guide?"

"Yes, something like that." I chewed on my thumbnail, worried he was going to decline.

"What time will I be meeting you at the ferry?"

I smiled.

CHAPTER TWENTY-FIVE

I TOOK THE FERRY over to the mainland, and Daniel was waiting for me by his car when I walked down the dock. With that disarming smile on his handsome face, he opened the door of his snazzy little sports car for me, and I got in.

"So, where are we off to?"

I pulled out the list of businesses I needed to visit. "Let's see…Queen of Tarts, Full Metal Works, Frontenac Jewels and Gems, Thunderbirds Art Gallery, and Gervais Floral Boutique."

"Well, you're in luck. Except for Full Metal Works, they are all in the same general vicinity in the downtown area. Full Metal Works is about a fifteen-minute drive south."

"Thank you for doing this."

"It's no problem. Gives me a chance to show off my town and spend time with you and visit my constituents all at once." He started the car and pulled out of the small parking lot. "After we do our runs, I'll take you to dinner at my favorite seafood restaurant right on the water."

We drove out to the metal-works company first. Daniel accompanied me inside and talked with the owner while I dropped off Samuel's contract. Then we went back downtown, and Daniel parked his car in his spot at the town hall, and we walked to the rest of the businesses. I didn't mind. It was one of those perfect late afternoons where the sun was starting its descent, but it was still warm with a cool but light breeze coming off the lake.

We hit Queen of Tarts next, which was a quaint little pastry shop with a tiny Ukrainian woman in charge named Corinne. She flirted with Daniel, then gave us both a cherry tart for free. I devoured it in two bites, it was so mouth-watering. Then we went into Frontenac Jewels and Gems, a large jewelry store with some very cool pieces that I eyed but walked away from because of the price.

After that, we visited Thunderbirds Art Gallery, which showcased local Objiwe artists. The last place we went to was Gervais Floral Boutique. The owner, Brittany, shook my hand, but her gaze never left Daniel's face. I knew that look. It screamed, "You are one handsome man!" I didn't blame her. Daniel *was* a very handsome man.

When all the paperwork had been delivered, Daniel led me down the public pier to a wooden house at the end. The sign out front read *Fisherman's Hook*, and underneath that: *If It Swims We Have It.*

"Cute," I said.

"Francois, the chef, is an artist. I promise you the best seafood you'll ever eat."

"That's a tall order. I am from California, remember?"

He made a face. "The best seafood comes from fresh water. Everyone knows that."

I laughed as he opened the door for me, and we went in. The hostess greeted Daniel by name, then led us to a table outside on the deck by the water. It was a beautiful spot with nothing impeding the view of the vastness of Lake Michigan.

After we ordered, we did the usual starter conversations—how long he'd been mayor, what drew him to politics, how did I like living at the Park Hotel, and how did I like being a concierge…

Which led to a conversation about why Samuel Park was torturing me.

"And you think that's why Mr. Park is testing you? Because your boss was an embezzler?"

"Yeah, he must think I'm going to embezzle funds from the hotel or something. Maybe he even thinks I helped Jeremy."

"That's ridiculous. You're a victim in all of that."

"I know, right?" I laughed, but more out of frustration than humor. "Jeremy Rucker has a lot to answer for. He ruined several lives in his pursuit of power and prestige, but that's not what brought him down in the end."

"No? What was it, then?"

I shook my head because it was still hard for me to believe, even though I knew it was true. What I kicked myself for, every day, was that I'd missed it. Totally. "He had a gambling problem. He dug himself into a hole and couldn't get out. He stole the money thinking he'd pay it back. But of course, he couldn't."

"I've known men like that." Daniel's gaze faltered, and he took a drink of wine to shield himself from whatever memory Jeremy's story had conjured. There was something there, something he didn't want to share. I wouldn't pry.

I finished my whitefish, and yes, it was as delectable as promised, and then pushed my plate to the side. "That was amazing."

"Told you."

"That you did." I picked up my wineglass and observed Daniel over the rim. He was definitely an attractive man, but over the course of the dinner, I came to realize that he was also smart, witty, and surprisingly well grounded. I suspected that came from his solid upbringing with a construction-working father and stay-at-home mother. Midwestern values, they called it. Daniel had them in spades.

"So, what about your family?" he asked. "Do you have siblings?"

I shook my head. "I'm an only child. My parents live in Hong Kong, and I don't see them much."

His eyebrows lifted. "What are they doing there?"

"I honestly don't know half the time. But they own and operate a private club. Club Paradise. It keeps them very busy." I finished off my wine and set the glass down, probably harder than I'd planned.

"Sounds exciting. How did they end up owning a private club in Hong Kong, of all places?" He seemed genuinely interested, not merely curious.

I took a deep breath and gave him the short version. "Well, when I was fifteen, Mom and Dad were managing a private club in a suburb near Detroit. We lived nearby. One of the frequent guests owned Club Paradise. When he needed a new manager, he made Dad an offer he couldn't refuse. Chance of a lifetime, my parents called it. They jumped in with both feet and never looked back. About ten years later, the owner died and my parents bought the place."

"Have you ever considered moving to Hong Kong?" he asked.

I forced a laugh. "Have you been talking to my mother?"

He shook his head.

"Well, no," I replied. "Living in Hong Kong is one of the last things I'd ever want to do."

Daniel frowned. "You're not close with your parents, I take it."

"No, but that's okay. I was raised by a lovely woman I've always called Miss Charlotte. She was a wonderful mother figure for me. I was lucky to have her in my life as long as I did."

He smiled. "You see her still?"

I shook my head. "Not in a few years, but I write to her as often as I can. She loves to get letters in the mail."

"Letters?" He arched his eyebrows.

"She says a phone call is nice, but then what do you have? Letters are proof she can hold in her hands that I've taken the time to send her my love. She says she re-reads them frequently." I smiled. "She made sure I learned perfect penmanship so she could actually read them."

"And do you have perfect penmanship?"

I made a face as I dug into my purse and pulled out a pen and a small notebook that I always carried to make my lists. I opened to a new page and wrote:

The quick brown fox jumps over the lazy dog.

Then I handed it to him.

He laughed as he read it. "Yes, that is quite perfect."

"Thank you very much. I practiced every day for years." Then I laughed. It felt good to share this with him. It felt good being here with him. It had been way too long since I had connected with a man. I'd been so busy with my career, climbing the ladder, reaching for the brass ring, that I hadn't made time for this. Whatever this turned out to be.

As we indulged in crème brûlée, we talked about this and that. Daniel regaled me with charming stories about his golden retriever, Max, and I told him about Scout and Jem and how much I missed them. He told me about kayaking on the lake and his spelunking trip to Carlsbad Caverns in New Mexico. I shared my love of sudoku puzzles and told him about the trip I'd taken with a friend to Bermuda after I graduated summa cum laude from Stanford Law.

By the time we left the restaurant, we were laughing about Daniel's dad and his older brother, Joshua, and their disastrous fishing trip that left them both in the water and their fishing poles at the bottom of the lake.

I was feeling very relaxed when we walked down the pier and back onto State Street, which was the main road through downtown Frontenac City. It was nearly seven o'clock, and I had to catch the last ferry back to the island soon.

"Thank you for dinner, Daniel. And for helping me deliver those contracts."

"It was my pleasure. Maybe we can do it…"

I didn't hear the last part of his sentence. My attention was on something across the street. Well, not something. Someone.

"Andi? Are you all right?"

I looked at him. "Huh?"

"Are you all right? You look like you've seen a ghost."

Not a ghost. But a very suspicious-looking grocery delivery boy walking quickly down the sidewalk, then ducking into an alleyway. What was he doing here?

I grabbed Daniel's hand and, tugging him along, jogged across the road.

"Indulge me," I said to him as his eyebrows popped up. But he didn't say anything and let me lead him along until we stopped at the mouth of the alley.

I peered around the corner to see Todd from the D&W duck down the next street. I pulled Daniel into the alley.

"Where are we going?" he asked.

"I'm not sure." I pointed to the far end of the alley. "What's there?"

He frowned as he thought. "I think a pawn shop. Yes, it's Lou's Pawn Shop. The front entrance is on the other end of the block, on Cadillac Street."

"Then that's where we're going."

We walked along the alley and around the corner. I pressed myself up against the brick wall and peered into the window of the shop. I didn't immediately see Todd, but then he stepped into view as he spoke with the man behind the long, glass case that doubled as a sales counter.

Daniel said, "Is there something you're not telling me? Like, you're actually a secret spy or something?"

"No, nothing like that," I replied without dropping my gaze from the scene inside the shop. "Just a concerned citizen."

Then it must've dawned on him, because he said, "Is this like when you were trying to find out who killed Thomas Banks? And you were asking me twenty questions?"

I shrugged. "Maybe?"

"Didn't you almost get killed trying to investigate that murder?"

"That's totally an exaggeration. I don't think I would've died from a blow to the head."

"But isn't that what killed that guy?"

The door to the shop opened. I pushed Daniel back into the alley, behind the wall, and squished up next to him to hide. I counted to ten then peered around the corner. Todd had left the shop, and I could see him walking along the street. It looked like he was maybe heading back to the ferry docks.

"Okay." I stepped out onto the street. "You stay here."

"Where are you going?"

"Into the pawn shop," I said. "He's up to something, and I'm going to find out what it is."

CHAPTER TWENTY-SIX

DANIEL GRABBED MY ARM before I could go running off into the pawn shop. "What is going on, Andi? Tell me the truth."

"The kid that was just in there is somehow involved in the murder of a woman named Ida Walker."

"How do you know for sure?"

"Because he was at her home on the morning she died. He delivers her groceries, and when I got there, the groceries were still on the counter and not put away. His name's Todd. He told the sheriff that he had to rush out after delivering. But what was the hurry? Also, items from her house have been missing. According to Mrs. Walker's great-nephew, Peter, did confess some of that stuff was taken by his own wife."

Daniel made a face. "Are you sure you're not reading too much into things?"

I shrugged. "Maybe. But I know this kid's girlfriend has been spotted on the streets selling old jewelry and stuff like that.

Maybe Todd stole something more valuable than that." I gestured to the store. "Hence, his visit to the pawn shop."

"That's kind of a big 'maybe,' don't you think? What if he's just pawning off some old electronics of his own or something?"

"You wait here, okay? I don't want to get you involved."

He dropped my hand, and I opened the door of the pawn shop and walked in. The little bell above the door tinkled pleasantly. The man behind the glass case smiled as I approached. He rubbed at his red, bulbous nose.

"How can I help you, miss?"

"I was wondering about the guy who was just in here."

"What about him?"

"What was he selling?"

He shook his head. "I can't tell you that. My customers expect privacy."

I could've told him all about privacy laws and the long list of things they don't protect, including selling stuff to pawn shops. Instead, I reached into my purse and took out a twenty-dollar bill from my wallet. I slapped it onto the counter.

The guy swiped the bill off the glass faster than a speeding bullet. "He comes in to sell jewelry sometimes."

"What was he selling today?"

He shrugged. "Not sure."

I slapped another twenty onto the counter. He swept that one up in his ham-sized fist, and then he pointed to a pair of earrings in the display case.

"Those."

I looked down in the case and studied the earrings. I didn't know Mrs. Walker well enough to know whether they belonged to her or not. Sighing, my gaze moved over the rest of the case, and then it locked onto something that I was certain belonged to her. A pearl necklace.

I pointed to it. "Did he sell you that?

"Can't remember."

"Let me see it."

I didn't think he was going to, because he looked at me for a long moment, chewing on the ends of his handlebar mustache. Then he unlocked the case and brought out the velvet box the necklace was lying in.

At first blush, it looked like any pearl necklace. But I'd studied the photos in Mrs. Walker's home. I'd noticed that one of the pearls of the necklace was slightly pinker than the other whiter ones. Before he could protest, I picked up the case and held it up to the light. I tilted it to the right then the left, and then stopped when I could clearly see the pink pearl. Careful not to actually touch the necklace, I set the case back down on the counter. I figured it already had too many fingerprints on it, and I hoped a few of them were Todd's.

"How much?" I asked.

"Five hundred."

I narrowed my eyes at him. "How much *really*?"

"For you, five hundred. Cash only."

I dug around in my purse and took out the envelope Mr. Lawson had given me for a tip. I counted the cash I had left. Three hundred fifty bucks. I couldn't believe I was going to do this. But I needed that necklace. It was evidence.

"How about three fifty?"

He shook his head. "We can stand here all night, but the price isn't going to change. Take it or leave it."

"You're being quite the ass."

"Hey, that's business."

I marched out of the shop. Daniel met me at the door. "What's going on?"

I sighed and then bit on my lower lip. "You wouldn't happen to have one hundred fifty dollars on you, would you?" Then I explained to him why I was asking.

Daniel grabbed my hand, and together, we went into the pawn shop. The proprietor raised his eyebrows as Daniel loomed over the counter. "Do you know me?"

"Sure do, Mr. Mayor."

"Then you are well aware that I speak regularly with the zoning committee and the chamber of commerce. I might even be meeting them tomorrow to go over new regulations for various shops downtown here."

"That's blackmail," he blustered.

"That's business." Daniel gestured to the necklace on the counter. "Now, how much is that going to be for my friend here?"

"Four hundred."

"I think you can do better than that."

"Three fifty."

Daniel cocked an eyebrow. "Are you sure it's that much?"

The proprietor groaned. "C'mon, you're killing my profit."

"How much did you give the kid for it?"

"Two hundred." He sighed and rubbed at his mustache.

I took out the money and put it onto the counter, then used a tissue to grab the case, snapped it shut, and put it into my purse. "Nice doing business with you."

When we were outside again, I jump-hugged Daniel. "Thank you." He pressed his hands against my back and held me there, and my heart did a little jig. I breathed him in. He smelled really good.

"You're welcome." He smiled. "But now you're out two hundred bucks."

I shrugged. "If this turns out to be the evidence I think it is, I don't mind at all."

He shook his head. "You're a wonder."

"Like in *wonderful*? Or as in you *wonder* what the hell I'm doing?"

He laughed. "Maybe a bit of both."

"I'll accept that."

The sun had dropped low in the sky, and it was time to catch the ferry back to Frontenac Island. Even though I really didn't want to.

"I'm sorry I ruined the evening."

"You didn't ruin a thing." He reached over and drew a strand of hair away from my cheek. The touch of his fingertip sent a buzz of electricity down my body. "I like you, Andi Steele, concierge of the Park Hotel, part-time detective."

"I like you, too, Mayor Evans." *Full-time hottie.*

He offered his arm, and I took it. "It's getting late. I'll drive you to the ferry."

At the port, Daniel walked me up the ramp to the ticket booth. After I paid for my ticket, I turned to face him, suddenly nervous. I bit down on the inside of my cheek and had to stifle a yelp.

"Will you text me when you get back to the hotel?"

I nodded. "Yeah. I will."

"Good." He stuck his hands in his jeans pockets. He looked almost as nervous as I felt. Which I didn't think was at all possible. What did he have to be nervous about? Did he not own a mirror? He was drop-dead gorgeous, successful, charming, and he smelled good. He was beyond a "catch." I, on the other hand, was a bit of a mess.

"So, thanks for everything," I said.

"You're welcome."

I started to walk down the dock to the ferry, but whirled around, marched back, grabbed Daniel's face in my hands, and kissed him full on the lips. His eyes widened, but thankfully, he didn't freak out. When I pulled back, he just smiled.

"Okay, 'bye," I said, then walked away quickly to the ferry. I didn't turn around again, although I desperately wanted to.

Once I was on the ferry, I went up to the top deck and looked out. Daniel was standing in the same spot where I'd left him on the dock. He waved when he saw me. I waved back, feeling my cheeks go red. I'd never done anything that spontaneous in my life. Surprisingly, it felt amazing and not out of control, which I always thought spontaneity was—a lack of self-control.

I pressed my fingers to my lips. They still tingled. The aftereffects of a lovely kiss. I kicked myself for not making it longer. I hoped I'd get another chance to kiss Daniel. I hoped I hadn't scared him off.

Since it was such a beautiful evening, I stood at the railing looking out at the water for most of the trip. Lost in my thoughts, I didn't hear when someone came up beside me to stand at the railing. But I did smell him—he had a greasy odor clinging to him. Like he'd been dipped in an old, dirty deep fryer.

I turned to see Todd glaring at me with bloodshot eyes.

"Are you following me?" he demanded.

"No, of course not. I don't even know you," I said sternly, with a little white lie on the side.

He took a step back. I'd obviously startled him a little. "Oh, I thought I saw you outside of…" He shook his head. "Never mind."

"Are you okay? You seem a bit on edge." Maybe I could get him talking. He looked like a kid into something way over his head. I'd heard that confession was good for the soul.

He took another step away. "I'm fine."

"Don't you work at D&W?"

His eyes narrowed. "Yeah? I thought you said you don't know me."

"I don't. Just I recognize you from there. You delivery the groceries, right?"

"Yeah, sometimes." He rubbed at his mouth. I noticed his lips were severely chapped, as if he'd been licking them a lot. "What's with all the questions?"

Although I'd worked in the corporate world, I had a friend from law school who had gone the public-defender route. I'd helped her out on a couple of cases from time to time. Down at her offices, I'd encountered several different types of people. They only qualified for a public defender if they couldn't pay for a lawyer. Which mostly meant hard-working people and those who were falling through the cracks for a variety of reasons. I had quickly learned to recognize signs of intoxication and drug addiction.

Todd was exhibiting a few of those signs.

"I was just thinking about home delivery service, that's all. Thought you could give me the skinny on it."

"You order some groceries, and I deliver them. Nothing more to it than that."

"Right." I nodded. "So, you would knock on my door and give them to me? What if I wasn't home? How would you deliver them?"

"We'd arrange a specific time."

I nodded again. "That makes sense. Do you ever deliver to the disabled? You know, folks who can't get out much? Like people with disabilities...or sometimes the elderly?"

He stared at me, his jaw clicking back and forth. His agitation level had jumped up.

"Would you have a key to go inside? Would you put away the groceries?"

I knew I was pushing him. Sheriff Jackson would definitely chastise me for this. But I didn't plan to tell him. I would simply deliver the necklace and be on my way—no mention of this conversation with Todd.

As the ferry neared the island, the captain's voice rang over the loudspeakers, instructing everyone about docking procedures.

Todd rubbed at his face again. His hands shook a little. "I've got to go." Then he walked away and rushed down the ladder to the main level.

I debated going after him. He seemed a bit unstable, though. I'd already had an iron skillet swung at me this week. I didn't need anything else threatening to whack me. I liked my body undamaged.

I stayed up top and watched Todd as the ferry docked. Once the ship was tied up and the ramp was lowered, he started walking down the dock. As he walked, he glanced once over his shoulder. I met his gaze. Then he turned around, hands fisted, walking with determination. I'd seen my share of guilty people. And Todd was most definitely guilty of something. Question was, what exactly had he done?

CHAPTER TWENTY-SEVEN

ONCE I WAS OFF the ferry, I headed toward the sheriff's station. I needed to drop off the necklace as soon as possible. I couldn't be walking around with it in my purse.

As usual, Deputy Shawn was the one who greeted me when I walked in.

He smiled, but he was never that friendly to me. I always felt like he was looking down his nose at me. Like I was a nuisance or something. If I hadn't been employed by the Park Hotel, my reception would probably have been downright cold. "He's not here."

Was I that obvious? Yeah, probably. Whenever I walked in here, it was to see the sheriff. Which was one of the problems between me and Deputy Shawn. He wanted all the women in the world to be focused on him all the time.

"Will he be in tonight?"

"Nope."

I had a decision to make. I could leave the necklace with the deputy, submitting it as evidence. But would he take it seriously?

I would hope so, but I was wary about Deputy Shawn's abilities as a law enforcement officer. He seemed like one of those men who became a cop to impress the ladies. My other choice was likely going to get me in some serious trouble with the sheriff. But it wasn't like I hadn't been there before.

"Okay, thanks. Ask him to call me when he has a chance, okay?" I nodded at him and then left the station.

I had a bit of a walk ahead, but I didn't mind. Thankfully, I'd worn comfortable shoes. I made a pit stop at the Weiss Strudel House.

Twenty minutes later, I was standing on the porch of a cute, white bungalow with bright-blue trim. The decor didn't match the man who lived here, but I really didn't know him *that* well to make such a judgment. Maybe he was a bright-blue trim type of guy and I just didn't know it.

I knocked twice and waited. A few moments later, the door swung open.

"Hi." I tried a big smile. "I brought you strudel." I shoved the box of pastries at him.

Sheriff Jackson didn't return my smile, and he didn't take the offered box. He stepped out onto the porch, looked around, then glared down at me. "Why the hell are you on my doorstep?"

"I know. I'm sorry. But I had to talk to you. I have something you need to see."

"I have put up with a lot from you. I've indulged you on many occasions." He clenched his jaw. "But this, showing up at my home, is not okay. You've crossed a line, Ms. Steele."

Uh-oh, we were back to Ms. Steele and not Andi.

"Look, Sheriff, you may have 'indulged' me." Yes, I air-quoted. "But you have to admit I'm more than helpful to you. I have provided you with a lot of information you wouldn't normally have found out about. You would never have solved the Banks murder without me."

Probably.

His eyebrows went up at that. "Are you calling me incompetent?"

I bit my lower lip, tamping down the urge to scream at this stubborn man. "Of course I'm not calling you incompetent, Sheriff. You're good at your job. It's just that I have certain skills and alternative methods you need, and you hate the fact that you need them. You don't like relying on a civilian, like me, to do any part of your job." I sighed. This visit was clearly not going the way I had planned.

"Good evening, Ms. Steele." He stepped back to close the door.

"Wait." I stopped the door with my palm. "I have vital evidence in the Walker murder."

His eyes narrowed. "What?"

I reached into my purse and pulled out the blue velvet box, using the tissue again so as not to add my fingerprints to the mix. I wriggled it at him. "Do you want to know what's inside?"

I was surprised I didn't hear his teeth grinding as he glared at me. But then he opened the door and stepped to the side to allow me entrance. Smiling, I crossed the threshold, and he shut the door a little too hard behind me.

He led me into a cozy living room with a blue sofa and matching chair. The TV was on, a hockey game, and I noticed the beer bottle on the coffee table and the half-eaten slice of pizza. Whoops. I'd interrupted his supper. A sudden rush of remorse came over me. I shouldn't have shown up at his house without calling. I rubbed at my tight chest, considering turning around and leaving. But I figured that would be even ruder.

"So, what is it?" he gestured to the blue box in my hand.

I opened it and showed him. "I'm pretty sure this necklace belonged to Mrs. Walker."

He took the box and inspected the necklace. "How do you know?"

"I've seen a couple of photos in her house where she is wearing this necklace. In those photos, you can see that one of the pearls has a pinkish shade to it. It's not quite pearly white."

Sheriff Jackson lifted the box up to the light and moved it around just as I had at the pawn shop. His eyes widened, and I knew he'd seen the pink hue on the pearls and probably in Mrs. Walker's photos, too.

"Where did you find it?"

"At a pawn shop in Frontenac City."

He nodded. "I'm going to assume that this is going to be a long, involved story."

I frowned. "I wouldn't say *long*, exactly."

The sheriff went to the little table near the front entrance, pulled open a drawer, and took out a plastic evidence bag. He put the necklace box inside, sealed it, and using a thick marker he'd also procured from the desk, wrote down the date, what was inside, and I assumed the case number. When he was done, he looked at me again.

"Do you want a beer?"

"Ah, no," I said, thrown off guard. "No thank you."

"I'm going to get another beer, then we're going to sit down, and you're going to tell me everything."

He disappeared into the kitchen, and when he came back, he had a bottle of beer in one hand and a tall glass of ice water in the other. He handed me the water.

"Thank you."

He sat on the sofa and gestured for me to sit as well. I did, and after taking a sip, I set my glass of water onto the coffee table.

"Tell me."

So I did. I told him how I spotted Todd, whom I recognized from the D&W, going into the pawn shop, then how I went inside and asked the owner about Todd and what he had sold there. I spotted the necklace, sure that it was Mrs. Walker's, and bought it for two hundred bucks.

I left out Daniel's involvement.

He shook his head. "You spent two hundred?"

I shrugged. "I had to. I didn't want the pawn-shop guy to sell it before I could call you and get you down there."

"I respect the ingenuity."

"And now that it's evidence, I thought surely the department has the budget to pay a girl back for that ingenuity."

He chuckled. "I'll see what we can do."

I smiled. "Thanks."

He took a long pull on his beer. "This is good, but it doesn't necessarily prove the kid killed her. He could've pinched the necklace at any time. Just like Colleen Walker was taking things from her. I don't think the old lady noticed that her stuff was being stolen."

"Maybe she'd been wearing it when she fell down the stairs. Though I know she wasn't wearing it when we found her."

"We'll have to find out. Ask around. Ask her nephew, ask the people who knew her."

"Also, I'm pretty sure Todd's a drug addict."

The sheriff frowned. "How do you figure that?"

Here goes nothin'. I should have kept my mouth shut like I'd intended.

"Well, he seemed pretty on edge when I, uh, talked to him."

He set the bottle onto the table with a loud clink. "You didn't mention that you talked to him."

"Yeah, on the ferry back to the island." I rubbed at my arm, chills suddenly rippling over my skin. "He kind of confronted me. Thinking he saw me following him to the pawn shop."

"Andi. Jesus. You're going to get yourself hurt."

At least we were back to *Andi* and not *Ms. Steele.*

"It was fine. I convinced him that he was confused. But he seemed really out of it. He was definitely high. Had the shakes. Wouldn't surprise me if he was a junkie. Or has a history of it."

He sat back on the sofa and scratched at the dark stubble on his chin. "I'd already pulled the sheet on him after finding out he was the delivery guy for Mrs. Walker. He does have a drug charge from last year."

"There you go."

"Doesn't mean he killed her."

"I know, but at least you have a good reason to pull him in for further questioning, with the necklace and all."

He nodded. "Yeah."

I took that moment to look around the room and sneak some peeks into the sheriff's personal life. The room was simple but tastefully decorated. There were a few paintings on the walls and lots of photos. I wondered if the decorating was left over from his ex-wife. I didn't know what happened there and wasn't going to ask. The place suited him, though. Clean lines, no muss, and no fuss.

He cleared his throat, bringing me back to the moment. "I'm sorry I was..."

"An ass?"

"Yeah, an ass. I value my privacy. As I'm sure you do as well."

"I do, yes. I'm sorry I showed up unannounced. I should've called."

"Yeah, you should have."

"Okay, well, now that we've thoroughly chastised each other, I should probably go."

He stood at the same time I did. I went to move past him and kind of bumped into him. He reached out to steady me, so I didn't fall ass over end onto the coffee table. The slight touch on my arm sent a surprising jolt of warmth over my skin.

Seemed like I'd been jolting all day—because of two different men, no less. Maybe I did need to spend some time on my personal life after all.

Then the front door opened, and Megan lurched in, dropping her purse and bag and kicking off her shoes all in one seamless motion. Her eyes bugged out when she spied us at the sofa, limbs sort of entangled.

"Oh my God, did I just interrupt something?" She put her hand over her mouth, trying to cover the laughter spilling out. "Were you two making out?"

We literally pushed away from each other and said in unison, "No!"

I blushed, he scowled, then I was grabbing my purse from the coffee table, nearly knocking over the beer bottles, and heading toward the door. "Goodnight. Thanks for the water." Then I was out the door, shutting it behind me, and marched down the steps of the porch.

The door opened again, and Sheriff Jackson came out. "Hold up, Andi."

I spun around, afraid my cheeks were still aflame. "Yes?"

"I don't feel right about you walking back to the hotel by yourself in the dark."

"I'll be fine."

"Colleen Walker was released earlier today, and she's got a bad temper. Now this Todd kid. Let me drive you."

I considered declining the offer, but I was a bit unnerved, and it wasn't because of the sheriff. On the ferry, Todd had frightened me a bit. He didn't look like a person in control. I felt sure he didn't know who I was or where to find me, but I couldn't be one hundred percent certain of that.

I nodded. "Okay. Thanks."

The short drive to the hotel felt like an eternity. I didn't know why I was nervous. I had no reason to be, but that thought didn't stop the butterflies in my belly. What was going on?

"I'm sorry about Megan," the sheriff finally said as he pulled up to the lobby of the hotel to drop me off.

"Don't be. It's fine."

"Sometimes she just blurts things out without thinking."

I put my hand on the door handle. "Seriously, no harm done. She just saw the wrong end of the stick."

He nodded. "Yeah, she definitely did." He scratched at his stubble again. "It was stupid to think that we'd ever, that we even…"

"Right. Stupid." I opened the door and got out. "Goodnight, Sheriff."

"Goodnight."

I didn't watch as he drove away but marched head high into the hotel. The staff nodded to me as I crossed the lobby toward the corridor to my suite. As I neared my door, I rubbed a hand over my belly. The butterflies were still at it. I didn't know why my body was reacting this way. It wasn't like I was at all attracted to Sheriff Jackson. He was a hard, stubborn man who definitely didn't like me all that well. So, why did I all of a sudden feel angry about his "stupid" comment? It *was* definitely stupid, the thought of us being together.

Wasn't it?

CHAPTER TWENTY-EIGHT

I GOT UP AT five instead of six in the morning, to be down at the desk an hour earlier than normal. The Park Hotel was expecting a VIP. Mrs. Willetta Garfinkel, the eighty-two-year-old widow of a wealthy hotelier and casino owner, was expected to arrive around nine with her assistant, Petra, and her French bulldog, Duchess. It was a huge deal, and everyone was expected to be in the lobby to greet her. She'd been making the trip every year at this time for the past ten years since her husband's death. Before that, they arrived together and got the royal treatment as a couple.

Two weeks ago, I'd received her list of requests for her month-long stay to make sure everything was ordered in and prepared ahead of time. The fridge in her suite was filled with spring water bottled in Colorado, which she used to brew her favorite brand of tea in ginger, mint, and green tea flavors. I'd arranged that a freshly baked scone with locally made strawberry preserves, two hard-boiled eggs, and freshly squeezed orange juice be delivered to her door every morning at exactly 7:30 a.m.

I had to admit these were not even near the most unusual or demanding requests I'd received working as concierge. They were actually pretty standard for a VIP of her stature. She didn't ask for anything too weird.

At ten past nine, the lobby doors opened and in walked Willetta Garfinkel. She was an elegant woman wearing an orange head wrap, with strands of lavender hair peeking out, and round sunglasses that covered most of her seriously gorgeous face. Her strides were long and sure, her lime-green silk pants billowing with each step. I had to admire any woman walking effortlessly in purple stilettos. I also admired her fashion sense. I was lousy at both stilettos and fashion, so there was absolutely no danger that I'd upstage her in any way.

Behind her marched a younger woman, probably in her thirties. She wore a sharply tailored suit I would've killed for in my lawyer days. I would've had clients eating out of my hands in that suit. It had *feminine power* written all over it. She carried a small tan dog in her arms. The assistant, Petra, bearing Duchess the Frenchie, I assumed.

Mrs. Garfinkel strode up to Samuel Park and smiled, her ruby-stained lips curling up with easy pleasure. "Hello, Samuel."

He clasped her hand and leaned in to kiss her pale cheek. "You look radiant as always, Willetta."

"Thank you. A month in a Swedish spa will do that for you. You should try it."

Lois stepped forward and shook Mrs. Garfinkel's hand. "It's a pleasure to see you. We're very happy you're staying with us again."

"Nice to see you, Lois." Her gaze swept over Eric and Nicole, and she smiled politely at them. Then she grinned at

Ginny. "You, I remember. You helped me find that amazing pair of tangerine jeans. I still wear them."

"I'm pleased to hear that, Mrs. Garfinkel," Ginny smiled.

Samuel gestured to me. "This is the new concierge, Andi Steele."

I shook her petite hand. "I'm honored to be able to serve you during your stay here at the Park Hotel."

"Where's the other one, the boy with the teeth?"

I pressed my lips together to suppress a grin. Casey did indeed have big teeth, and he constantly flashed them with his big cheesy smile, which I assumed he thought was charming and not smarmy. Wrongly so.

Samuel said, "He's taking care of his mother. She recently had hip surgery. It's a shame he's not here."

Mrs. Garfinkel gave a little shrug and looked at me again. "She looks more than capable. The job's not all that difficult, after all."

I nodded to her, not completely sure she'd paid me a compliment. "Thank you, ma'am."

"Your bags are already in your suite," Samuel said as he literally fluttered at the woman's side.

"Excellent." She waved her hand, and the entourage moved past me, now with Samuel and Lois in tow.

I watched the parade until they disappeared down the right corridor leading to the private elevator to the luxury suites on the third floor. When they were gone, Ginny came up to me.

"She's something, eh?"

"Yeah, not what I expected at all."

"If I'm half as pretty and vibrant as she is at that age, I'll be set for life."

"You'll be just as funky, Ginny, at eighty-two. I have no doubt in my mind." I laughed when she hugged me.

"Oh, you always say the right thing, you silver-tongued minx. That's why you're perfect for this job."

Everyone went back to their proper positions, and by the time noon rolled around, I had booked fifteen dinner reservations around the island, two sunset cruises, and three rounds of golf…and saved one toddler from running out of the hotel and getting on a tour carriage for bird-watching enthusiasts.

During a lull between guests, I ran over to the Lady Slipper for my usual veggie wrap and bottle of Kombucha. As I uncapped the bottle, I thought about Daniel and the day I'd spilled my tea all over his shoes. Not the most perfect meet-cute, but it got the ball rolling.

Since our dinner on the mainland, he'd texted me a few times to chat. I liked the casual nature of it. I didn't like a man who was all in after one date. That was never authentic. I liked a man who took his time.

Then that made me think of Sheriff Jackson, and I frowned. I didn't want to be thinking about the sheriff in any capacity except for law enforcement. I didn't want to think about him in his pretty blue house and going out for lunch with his daughter or the way he ran a hand through his hair when he was stressed.

Suddenly angry, I stomped across the lobby toward the back employee office to eat my lunch. I must've looked like I might punch through a wall, because the Chamber Crew—the hotel maids—moved out of my way as I strode past them.

"Man troubles?" Nancy asked with a smirk. The other women all laughed. Including Megan.

"No. I'm not having man troubles."

"That's not what we heard." Nancy snorted.

I glanced at Megan. "Really, Megan? After I helped you? You're going to spread extremely false rumors about me?"

She shrugged but had the decency to look chagrinned, at least. "Sorry. Just having some fun."

"Well, it's not fun for me. Or for your dad."

Nancy waved her hand. "Oh, relax, Steele. It's not like anyone would really believe that a man like Sheriff Jackson would have the hots for a woman like you."

I frowned. "What does that mean?" I put my hand on my hip, anger on the rise again.

She smacked me on the shoulder. "Don't get your panties in a twist. It's not an insult. It's just the sheriff is, you know, a rugged type of man. A man's man. Good with his hands." She winked at me. "And you're like, you know, educated and a bit uptight and probably scream when you see a spider." She laughed. "You're just really mismatched, that's all."

Nancy was absolutely right in her assessment, but I still felt stung. She hadn't meant to insult me. At least I didn't think so. Nancy and I got on pretty well. I had helped her a while ago with some troubles she'd been having with her ex-husband.

"I am not uptight," I said after a long pause, which made the crew laugh some more.

"You're just mismatched, is all," Nancy reiterated between giggles.

Everyone's a comedian.

I ate my lunch quickly and returned to the concierge desk. There were a couple of messages left on my desk from guests. One was from Mrs. Garfinkel. I immediately picked up the phone and called her suite.

She answered. "Yes?"

"Mrs. Garfinkel? It's Andi Steele, the concierge."

"Right. I need your help."

"Of course. How may I help you?"

"You need to come to my suite, right now."

"Is it an emergency? Do I need to bring someone from a different department, like housekeeping?"

"No. You'll do fine. Be here in five minutes." Then she hung up the phone.

I let the front desk know where I was going. Five minutes later, I was knocking on the double doors of the Frontenac Suite.

The doors opened. "Good. You're punctual. I like people who are on time."

I entered the front foyer of the best and largest suite in the hotel and followed Mrs. Garfinkel into the parlor. The suite was beautifully decorated in blue and white, little splashes of gold here and there. The white curtains were pulled away from the entire wall of windows that led to a verandah overlooking the water. She had a fine view of the magnificent bridge connecting the upper and lower peninsulas of Michigan, too. Spectacular.

"What can I help you with, Mrs. Garfinkel?"

"I need you to take Duchess for a walk."

The little dog in question trotted into the room and plopped its little butt near my feet.

"I was under the impression that your assistant, Petra, did all the dog-walking while you were here on the island."

"Petra is indisposed."

That was when I heard the very distinctive sound of someone retching in the bathroom. I winced at the sound. "Oh. Is she okay? Should I call for a doctor?"

She made a face. "She's fine. Just a horrible traveler. She'll be like this for a day or two. It's nothing serious."

Duchess moved a little closer to me. I tried not to make eye contact with the dog. I knew if I did, I'd be done for. I love dogs. But I've never been in a position to own one. Lois would have a heart attack if I brought a dog to live with me in my suite. She'd kick me out for sure. She wouldn't let me have my cats here, and they were a lot less likely to damage anything than a dog would be.

"You see, Duchess already likes you." Mrs. Garfinkel leaned down, attached the bedazzled leash to the dog's collar, and then handed it to me. "She has lots of energy. A good hour walk will help her calm down." She also handed me a bag. It looked like one a mother of a new baby would carry around her shoulder. "Everything you need is inside. I'll see you in an hour." She crouched and kissed the dog on its furry head. "Behave for Ms. Steele."

Duchess woofed softly, then led me to the door, obviously knowing exactly what she was supposed to do and why I'd been called. We walked to the lobby, where I informed the front desk that I'd be gone longer than planned. Everyone cooed at the dog.

Lane came around to pet Duchess. "You are so lucky to be walking her."

I nodded, taking his word for it. At least Duchess wasn't yappy. She was actually quite well behaved and extremely cute. I bet Daisy would die to cuddle her. So, I decided we'd walk down to the kennels for a visit. Maybe Duchess could even play with Lulu, and I could pop in and see Scout and Jem for some snuggles.

The walk down the hill to the village was a leisurely affair. Duchess stopped every five feet or so to smell everything low enough to smell. The normal ten-minute trip took twice as long with Duchess leading me all the way. She was small but sturdy, and she wouldn't move on from one smelling spot to another until she was darn good and ready.

But I was right. Daisy nearly lost her mind when I walked in with the French bulldog. Squealing, she jumped out of the chair at her desk and immediately got on the floor with Duchess. The dog obviously knew an animal lover when she smelled one, as her little butt wouldn't stop wiggling, and she couldn't lick Daisy's face fast enough.

"Oh my God, Duchess, you're so cute." Daisy kissed Duchess on the head and nose while cuddling her to her chest.

"You know her?"

"Yeah. A couple of times, I've been called up to the Park to watch her for Mrs. Garfinkel. Duchess is adorable. You're lucky to get to walk her," Daisy said.

I smiled. "That's what everybody says."

"Cool." Daisy gave the dog a few more kisses.

"Where's Lulu?" I asked. I thought the two dogs would probably get along.

"You'll never guess what happened?"

"What?"

"Mrs. Walker's will stated that Mr. Rainer should be given ownership of Lulu. The sheriff called me after he heard from the lawyer."

I lifted my eyebrows with fake surprise. "Wow. That is great news."

"He's going to be so happy."

I knew that was true.

Daisy's head came up suddenly, and she made an O with her mouth. "I have a great idea. Why don't you and Duchess come with me to deliver Lulu to Mr. Rainer? We could walk there. Would be great exercise for the pups."

And it would be a chance to vindicate myself. I still felt guilty about taking Lulu away from Mr. Rainer in the first place.

"That's a great idea."

CHAPTER TWENTY-NINE

THE WALK TO MR. Rainer's place took about twenty minutes. The two pups had a great time running around together, barking at inanimate objects and birds. By the time we got onto Mr. Rainer's street, though, Lulu was tired, and Daisy had to carry her the rest of the way. Duchess was still full of energy.

The two neighbor women, Blue and Sunglasses, were sitting in chairs on their front lawn as we passed by.

I waved to them. They waved back.

"Did you lock down that sheriff yet?" Blue asked as she sipped on her iced tea and waved a hot-pink fan at her face. She looked like a Southern Belle. Except the weather wasn't that hot right now. It was only around sixty-five degrees. And we were far from the southern states.

Daisy gave me a look, but I ignored it.

"Like I said before, I'm not interested in Sheriff Jackson. We're just colleagues."

"Yeah, that's what those Twilight kids always said," Sunglasses argued. "And look what happened there."

She was referencing a fictional couple, only one of which was a live human. Those two had ended up in an explosively bad relationship and endured a tragic breakup. Not a great analogy.

I had no intention of standing there and arguing with them about the sheriff. We continued our walk until we reached Mr. Rainer's porch. Daisy knocked on the door.

For a moment, I thought maybe Mr. Rainer wasn't home, but then he slowly cracked the door open and peered out. His deep frown was ripe with agitation until he saw Lulu tucked under Daisy's arm. Then he threw open the door and beamed like a kid at Christmas.

"She's all yours, Mr. Rainer," Daisy said. "I guess it was in Mrs. Walker's will."

He eyed me for a moment. I frowned and quickly shook my head—out of Daisy's line of sight, of course—warning him to play along that he was ignorant of the contents of the will. And then he was all gap-toothed smiles.

Daisy handed him the little Pekinese. Lulu perked up instantly when Mr. Rainer held her. She licked at his face while her tail wiggled back and forth. Daisy set a bag down on the ground beside him.

"I packed up some of the toys she was playing with at the kennel, some treats, a blanket, and a few coupons for dog food. I recommend you get food from me. All organic and not full of gross stuff. I'll deliver it to you. And I'm cheaper, too."

"Thank you," he said.

"Just take good care of her." Daisy petted Lulu's head. "She's precious."

"I will," he said with emotion in his voice.

I was about to apologize to him again about my interference when a loud crash from Mrs. Walker's house made us all turn.

"Is there someone over there?" I asked.

Mr. Rainer shrugged. "I think that lazy nephew of hers."

I handed Duchess's leash to Daisy. "Hold her for a minute." I rushed down Mr. Rainer's porch steps.

Daisy called out, "Andi, why are you going over there? Let's just call the sheriff."

"If I'm not out in fifteen minutes, you can call him."

I wasn't really sure why I was acting like I was some kind of gunslinger. Peter wasn't a stable guy. Since the contents of Mrs. Walker's will was now public, I suspected Peter had learned she hadn't left him a penny and he was pissed.

I'm an optimist. I also believed everyone deserved to be heard. Maybe he just needed someone to talk to, to really hear him. And maybe I could keep him from digging himself any deeper.

I went around to the kitchen entrance. The back door was unlocked. I opened it slowly and stepped inside.

The startling sound of breaking glass greeted me when something shattered against the wall in the next room. Glass bits rained down on the floor like hailstones.

"Peter?"

There was a grunt, then footsteps crunching on other broken things. Peter stuck his head around the corner and looked into the kitchen. His scowl was deep and a bit frightening.

"What do you want?" he demanded in an angry tone.

"You know you shouldn't be in here."

"Why do you care?" he snarled loudly.

"Because I think you are grieving."

"Grieving? Please. Don't make me laugh. We're all better off with her dead. She was a miserable old witch." He kicked one of the heavy wooden dining room chairs. It fell over with a loud bang.

"I'm hearing that more and more about her." I considered taking a step forward, but I didn't think it would be a good idea. I could feel the waves of violence coming off him. The best thing to do right now was to leave and call Sheriff Jackson like Daisy had said.

But, of course, I didn't. "I still think you're grieving. I think you cared a little, or you wouldn't have seen to her needs all these years. Right?"

He glared at me, but I sensed that I'd cracked his wall of anger, if only a little. He gripped the back of a chair, his knuckles turning white as he squeezed. A vein along his temple throbbed. I could see the vein pulse, even from where I stood. I really didn't want to witness another man collapse in front of me. It was unnerving, to say the least.

I moved toward him. "Peter, I'm sorry this is happening to you. But you have to see that what you're doing isn't helping matters. It only makes you look…"

"Guilty?"

"Yes. Actually."

"I didn't kill my aunt."

I did the only sensible thing. I lied. "I know you didn't kill her."

He glared at me, but he didn't throw anything.

I pushed onward. "But destroying her home? You're just giving the sheriff more and more reasons to think that you killed her. Your wife's past behavior hasn't helped, either."

He let out a long sigh, and his grip on the chair lessened a little. "I'm angry."

"Of course, you are." I nodded. "It's understandable under the circumstances."

"Colleen wanted to come here at night and just pack up everything from the house and take it and sell it."

"Your wife doesn't have the brightest ideas. Her time in jail should be proof of that."

He nodded, and I could see the exhaustion of the past tumultuous week crushing him. I felt sorry for him. I knew what it was like to have some unexpected event completely destroy your life. When it had first happened to me, I felt absolutely lost and hopeless. If it hadn't been for Ginny, I wasn't sure I would've come through it all. It was obvious Peter didn't have anyone he could rely on, to confide in. No one to help him through the tough times.

"I don't know what to do," he finally said, his voice low, wavering a little.

"When I went through something horrible a few months ago, I didn't know what to do, either. My whole life had come apart, and I felt completely helpless. But then I did something I didn't think I could do. I packed up what was left of my tattered life, and I moved here."

"Why?"

"Because I could start fresh and create a different life for myself." I crept forward cautiously and stood next to him at the dining room table. "Is there anything keeping you here now? Maybe moving to a different city or town would do you some good."

He frowned. "A buddy of mine works up in Alaska on an oil rig. He always tells me they are looking for guys to hire."

"Sounds like a good opportunity."

He nodded and then sighed again. "Maybe. I'd have to convince Colleen."

"Working on the rigs is shift work, isn't it? Ten days on, five days off, something like that?"

"Yeah, something like that."

"She wouldn't have to move with you. I've known couples who've done this. It's a great way to make money for the household," I said, not adding that it would be a great way for him to get away from Colleen. Proximity to her was at least some of his problem.

He rubbed at his face. He seemed to be considering it.

"Besides, she's stuck here for a bit, I think. With the legal trouble she's gotten herself into. You'll need the money to help her, too," I said.

He nodded. He no longer held the chair in a death grip. I hoped he was thoroughly defused. When he spoke, his tone was almost normal again. "I should've known that girl would get Colleen into trouble. I told her we should've gone to the sheriff right away."

"What girl?" His shift of topic confused me.

"Hannah."

"The clerk from the D&W?"

He nodded. "Colleen knows her older sister. They went to high school together."

"What does Hannah have to do with all of this?"

"That's where Colleen got the idea to take stuff from Aunt Ida and sell it."

"What? Hannah suggested you steal from your great-aunt? Why?"

"I guess she used to come with her boyfriend on his delivery rounds. She knew Aunt Ida owned stuff that might bring in a few bucks." He shook his head. "That girl is more trouble than she's worth. Her sister is the same. I could never understand why Colleen hung around her. She was always up to no good."

I stared at him. I wondered if Hannah had been here with Todd to deliver groceries on the day Mrs. Walker died. That was something the sheriff should investigate.

Peter rubbed his face again. "Thank you for…being kind." Tears welled in his eyes.

"Hey, it's okay." Panic swelled in my chest. I didn't know what to do with a two-hundred-pound crying giant of a man.

He reached for me, and before I could dance out of the way, he pulled me to him and buried his face into the curve of my neck and sobbed. Off guard, unsure of what to do, I just patted his back and made soothing noises.

"It's okay. You'll be okay."

Then the front door opened, and Sheriff Jackson came in, his hand itching at his gun belt. Daisy must've called him since I'd been gone for more than the promised fifteen minutes.

I looked at him around Peter's tall body and shrugged as the big man continued to cry on my shoulder.

The sheriff shook his head but lowered his hand. Obviously, this wasn't a "draw the gun" type of situation any longer. I almost asked him to hand me the tissue box that was on the table near the front door—my shirt was getting a bit wet. But I held back on that request.

When Peter was done purging his bottled-up emotions, he dropped his arms and stepped away from me. He wiped at his eyes, then turned and noticed the sheriff standing awkwardly nearby. His cheeks flared with embarrassment.

"Everything's fine here, Sheriff Jackson. Right, Peter?"

Peter nodded.

The sheriff looked around at the damage. "Things don't look fine."

"Peter was just about to clean this all up when I interrupted him."

Peter gave me a look and then turned back to the sheriff. "That's right."

"So, you're saying it was like this when you got here, Peter?"

Peter visibly sagged and shook his head. "No. I did the damage. But I'll pay for it. All of it."

The sheriff's eyes narrowed as he assessed Peter. Then he nodded. "I won't charge you with destruction of property, but I'm going to hold you to your promise of paying for all the damages."

"Thank you, Sheriff."

"Andi, can I have a word?" He stepped out onto the front porch.

I joined him outside, even though I knew he was going to berate me for…well, it could be anything, really.

"Let me guess." I decided to preempt him. "You're going to ask, 'What the heck are you doing?' Then you're going to question my logic and point out my inability to stay out of things."

"Actually, I was going to let you know that I haven't been able to find Todd and that I've issued a warrant for his arrest. I want you to be cautious until we find him. And call me immediately if he should approach you." He rubbed his chin. "But, yeah, I like where you were going with that other stuff."

"Have you talked to Todd's girlfriend, Hannah? She's a checker at the D&W."

"We tried," he said. "She's not at work—day off—and she's not at home."

"I think she's involved in all of this."

He frowned. "Why do you say that?"

"Peter said that Colleen got the idea to steal Mrs. Walker's stuff from Hannah. I guess Colleen is friends with Hannah's older sister or something. Also, Hannah often accompanied Todd on his delivery rounds. If Hanna suggested Colleen steal from Mrs. Walker, she probably helped Todd do the same thing. Maybe that's where she got the idea to encourage Colleen to steal from Mrs. Walker in the first place."

His eyebrows went up. "That's an interesting theory."

"Maybe she was here that morning with Todd."

He nodded, pinching the bridge of his nose as if to ward off a headache. "Wish we had any kind of evidence to support that. Like a witness, for example."

I agreed, and then my gaze flitted to the yard across the street. Blue and Sunglasses were still outside, sitting in lawn chairs, both their gazes firmly directed toward this house—and Sheriff Jackson and me. I could see Blue's wide, cheeky grin even from here.

"We might have a couple of witnesses, actually."

He gave me a look, and I gestured toward the ladies. "Frontenac Island's most efficient neighborhood watch."

Chapter Thirty

BLUE AND SUNGLASSES BOTH perked up when they watched us cross the street and approach their front yard.

"I'll ask the questions," the sheriff said to me under his breath right before we stopped at the fence and, conveniently, right before I could respond.

"Good afternoon, Sheriff," Blue said flirtatiously from behind her pink fan.

"Afternoon." He tipped his hat, and they both nearly swooned. Then Sunglasses slid down her shades and gave me a knowing look, like, *See how handsome and gallant he is?*

"What brings you over to visit?" Blue asked.

"Andi tells me that you were out in your yard the morning of Mrs. Walker's unfortunate death."

Blue nodded. "I was pruning the roses."

"And you saw Colleen Walker?"

"Yup, saw her go in and come out pretty quickly."

I glanced at the sheriff—that matched up with what Peter had said.

"It was around eleven," Blue said.

Sunglasses nodded in agreement. "Yup, eleven. Ellen was on."

"Did you see anyone else enter Mrs. Walker's house that morning?"

They both made scrunched-up thinking faces, then Blue said, "Well, the delivery boy, of course. Todd. But he comes around almost every day. He delivers to a lot of the neighborhood."

"Was he here before or after Colleen Walker?"

"Before. Ten thirty maybe," Blue said.

"Was he alone?" I asked before the sheriff could. He gave me a hard look but didn't contradict me.

Sunglasses frowned. "Well, he had his helper with him, as usual."

"Yeah, pretty girl."

"Long blond hair?" I asked. They both nodded.

"Hannah. She's really sweet," Blue said. "Helps with the groceries. She helps me tidy the bedrooms sometimes."

Sheriff Jackson looked at me, and I suspected he had the same thoughts I had about Todd and Hannah. Could be Frontenac Island's very own Bonnie and Clyde.

"One last question, ladies," the sheriff said. "Have you noticed anything missing from your homes in the past few months? Jewelry, electronics, stuff like that?"

The two women glanced at one another, and then Sunglasses said, "Well, now that you mention it, I lost a pair of diamond earrings last month. It was one of the last gifts from my late husband. Fortieth wedding anniversary present. I was positive they were in my jewelry case. I hadn't worn them in years. When

I looked, they weren't there. No idea where I might have put them."

"And I lost the two hundred bucks I had stashed under the mattress. I probably spent it and forgot, though. I do that sometimes," Blue added.

Sunglasses gaped. "Do you think those two kids are responsible?"

The sheriff chewed on his lip for a second, then said, "I'd have someone else deliver your groceries and help with the cleaning from now on."

Blue fist-pumped the air. "I knew I wasn't losing my marbles." She pointed at Sunglasses. "I told you, Nora. I told you I didn't spend it."

Sunglasses waved her hand dismissively. "Kris, I didn't say you spent it."

"Yes, you did."

The sheriff cleared his throat, interrupting the argument that was about to erupt into years of bickering. "Thank you, Mrs. Gray and Mrs. Houston, for answering all our questions. You've been very helpful."

"Anytime, Sheriff." Blue flashed him a cheeky grin.

When he turned around to head back to his vehicle, Blue gestured to him, then to me, and then did something crude with her hands. Sunglasses burst out laughing.

I just shook my head at them and caught up with the sheriff across the street.

"So, you know those two, huh?"

"I'm the sheriff, and this is a very small island, Andi. I know everybody who lives here," he replied.

"And you're thinking Todd and Hannah are working a theft ring here in the neighborhood?"

He nodded. "It's a small, friendly neighborhood. Pretty much everyone's elderly. Prime targets for a couple of small-time thieving asshats."

I snort-laughed.

He looked at me oddly.

"Sorry. I've just never heard you talk like that."

"I'd call them worse, but not in refined company."

I scrunched up my face, wondering if he'd just complimented me. I could never be sure with him.

Daisy and Duchess met us at the sheriff's jeep. Would it be horrible to admit I'd totally forgotten about them and that they were waiting for me? Probably. So, I wouldn't admit it.

"Is everything okay?" Daisy asked.

I nodded. "Yeah, nothing to worry about."

She handed me Duchess's leash. "We should probably get back to the kennels."

"I'll drive you." Sheriff Jackson opened the door for us and then looked at me. "Then I'll take *you* back to the hotel."

When we arrived at Daisy's place, my cell phone rang. I dug it out of my purse and answered. "This is Andi." I waved to Daisy as she jumped out of the jeep.

"This is Willetta Garfinkel."

"Yes, Mrs. Garfinkel? What can I do for you?"

Duchess perked up in my lap. She must've heard her mistress's voice on the phone.

"Before you return, I'm wondering if you could do me another favor."

I held my finger up to Sheriff Jackson so he wouldn't pull away from the curb just yet. I had a feeling I was going to be making another stop before the hotel.

"Yes, of course."

"I'm afraid Petra is sicker than I originally thought, and I need you to pick up a prescription the doctor called in to the pharmacy on Main Street."

"Of course I will. Is there anything else you or Petra need?"

"Some Alka-Seltzer would be welcome."

"No problem. I'll be back in half an hour at most," I said.

"Thank you, Andi. You're a life saver."

We disconnected, and I put my phone back into my purse. I looked at the sheriff. "Mind if we make a quick stop to the pharmacy before heading to the hotel?"

"Sure. No problem."

He pulled away from the curb in front of the kennel then did a U-turn so we could head up Main Street. His radio crackled to life.

"Sheriff." It was Deputy Shawn.

He picked up the radio and pressed a button. "Go ahead."

"Got a report that Roger Clemons was streaking through the rec center again."

The sheriff shook his head and sighed. "Send Marshall."

"The rec center asked for you, Sheriff. You're the only one Roger will listen to."

Another deep sigh, then he looked at me.

"Go," I said. "I'll be fine."

"I'll be there in five minutes." The sheriff hooked the radio and then parked his jeep in front of the pharmacy to let me out.

"Have fun with your streaker." I opened the door.

"Hey, Andi, I appreciate how you handled Peter Walker today. It's not how I would've done it, but you got him handled, and I didn't have to arrest him. Which is always a win-win."

I smiled, my chest swelling with pride. "I'm going to take that as high praise, Sheriff." I jumped out of the jeep, shut the door, and placed Duchess onto the sidewalk. The sheriff drove away.

I collected Petra's prescription and the Alka-Seltzer, as well as some minty gum that might work because it always settled my stomach. Duchess and I set out to make the walk back up the hill to the Park. The little dog was getting tired. She wasn't quite as bouncy as before.

As we passed several shops and a busy restaurant, Duchess sniffed every entryway and just about every person in range. My cell phone rang. I stopped to get it out of my purse, saw that it was Daniel, and dropped the pharmacy bag. When I went to pick it up, I accidentally let go of Duchess's leash. After juggling everything again, while trying to answer the phone, I went to grab her leash, but she took off down the nearby alley.

Can nothing be simple?

"Hello? Andi?"

"Need to call you back. I'm having an emergency." I disconnected while he was still talking and took off after the dog.

"Duchess!" She was quick, a tan bullet whizzing down the lane. As I ran along the alleyway, my sandals slapping hard on the pavement—they were not made for sprinting—I spotted what she was chasing. A tabby cat.

She ran for another block and then stopped near an old wooden shack that was kind of tucked away in a corner. Once I caught up to her and grabbed her leash, I was breathing harder than I should have been. I was out of shape since I moved to the island, and it was getting to be a problem.

The dog was busy sniffing some weeds near the side of the ramshackle shelter. That must've been where the cat had vanished. The little house appeared abandoned. From the old sign still swinging over the door, it looked like it was once a fish-and-chips joint.

I reached Duchess in the weeds and gently pulled on her leash. "C'mon, it's time to go home and see your mommy." She looked up at me, panting.

As we turned to leave, I caught a whiff of something foul and fatty. It was an old smell. Of grease and things deep fried in dirty oil. The odor was strong and just about made me gag. Then it triggered something in my mind, and I paused and turned back to look at the shack.

Todd had that same rancid smell on him when he'd confronted me on the ferry. His father had told the sheriff that he hadn't been home in days. Was this where he was hiding out?

I surveyed the place, looking for a door. I found it on the other side. It was broken and nearly falling off the hinges. Through the crack, I could peer inside. The shack was empty save for much of the junk left behind by previous owners. I did spy a set of stairs on the outside that led up to an attic-type apartment above.

I scooped Duchess into my arms and then slowly crept up the stairs. Some of the weathered wood creaked and groaned under my weight, but I didn't think it would collapse. When I reached the top, I was able to peer into a grimy window beside a door. At first, I didn't see anything, but after a few moments, I saw movement. Someone was definitely inside.

My phone buzzed from my purse again. Juggling Duchess, I pulled it out. It was a text from Daniel.

Are you okay?

I'm fine.

You're doing something dangerous again, aren't you?

Got to go.

After turning my phone to silent mode and slipping it back into my purse, I pressed my ear to the flimsy, flaking wood door. Two distinct voices were arguing. I recognized them both. Todd and Hannah.

"Maybe we should turn ourselves in," Todd said.

"Are you stupid?" This from Hannah. "We'll both go to prison for the rest of our lives."

"It was an accident, though."

"No one's going to believe that. They'll think I pushed her on purpose."

I saw Todd grab Hannah's hand. "I'll tell them what happened. They'll see the bruises…"

"It won't matter. We have enough money now. We can get out of—"

Duchess barked. I guess she was getting bored of me standing there holding her.

Hannah looked toward the window. "Someone's outside."

Crap. That was my cue to get the heck out of there.

Clutching the dog, I rushed down the stairs, careful I didn't fall or put my foot through one of the rotting wood treads. The door opened up top, and Todd and Hannah came running after me. When I reached the bottom, Duchess jumped out of my arms. Before I could scoop her back up, Hannah grabbed her.

"What are you doing here?" she asked.

"Nothing." I reached for the dog. "Give my dog back, please."

Hannah pulled the dog out of reach, holding her tighter to her chest, which Duchess didn't like. She made a whining sound. "Not until you tell us what you're doing here."

"I know you from the ferry." Todd frowned and wiped at his nose. "You *were* following me."

"Look, let's all be calm here." I took a small step toward Hannah. "Put the dog down, and we can talk all this out."

She made a face. "You work for the sheriff?" Her agitation was scaring Duchess. The dog started to whimper in earnest. If she hurt that dog even one iota, I could kiss my job goodbye.

"I don't work for the sheriff. I'm just a concerned citizen." I took another tiny step forward. "I don't want to see you two throw your lives away."

"We'll go to jail for life," Hannah said. I could hear the waver in her voice. She was on the verge of something.

"Not necessarily. Cases like these aren't always cut-and-dry." I could almost reach out and grab Duchess, but I didn't want to spook Hannah and risk her crushing the poor pooch.

"It was an accident!" Todd shouted. "The mean old witch was hitting Hannah with her cane. Hannah defended herself, and Mrs. Walker fell. That's all. I swear."

I glanced over at Todd. He was bouncing from one foot to the other, clearly anxious and distraught.

"You need to talk to the sheriff, Todd. Tell him your side. Running away is not the answer. You'll be on the run for the rest of your life. It'll be impossible to live somewhere else with this hanging over you."

"Don't listen to her!" Hannah shouted. "We can do it. Let's go now!"

She went to turn, and I grabbed her arm and snatched Duchess. I bent to place the dog on the ground and out of the way when Todd rushed toward me. He looked like a raging linebacker intending to knock me onto the cement.

Before he could reach me, though, he was tackled to the ground by Sheriff Jackson. I don't know where he came from, but he moved like lightning, that was for sure. He flipped the kid over and straddled his back to put the cuffs on. None too gently, I noticed.

I thought for a second that Hannah was going to bolt, but she didn't. She just stood there looking down at her boyfriend and started to sob. I felt a bit sorry for her. It was clear—now that I was next to her and she wasn't smothered in makeup—that she'd suffered a few hits to her body. She had bruises on her upper arms, on her neck, and I could see the bruises that lingered on her cheek and just above her eye.

When the sheriff was done with Todd, he stood and handcuffed Hannah, a bit more gently than he had with Todd. He recited their rights to them after they were both secured and then sat her on the ground next to Todd.

He came over to me. "Are you okay?"

"Yes, I'm fine."

He looked me over, obviously not believing me. To his credit, I was often lying when I said I was fine. No one is ever really fine. I was shaken but didn't want to admit it. I'd put myself in danger, once again. In my defense, though, I'd done it to save Duchess.

The dog sniffed at my feet, then looked up at me and woofed. I reached down and picked her up. She licked my face. What a little sweetie she was.

Sheriff Jackson let loose a long, loud sigh. "This time I'm driving you straight to the hotel. No more pit stops."

I didn't argue. Pit stops seemed to be my demise.

CHAPTER THIRTY-ONE

INSTEAD OF WAITING FOR the sheriff to book Todd and Hannah at the station—I imagined it would take some time and I had to get Duchess home—I called Ginny to come pick me up. Sheriff Jackson had insisted. He didn't want me walking back alone.

I could've argued with him. I'd caught Mrs. Walker's killer, so I wasn't in danger anymore. But I had a feeling it was more than just that. He probably didn't want me to stumble upon another crime and embroil us all in another case. He kept telling me that Frontenac Island had never experienced a crime wave before I came to live here. Like it was my fault or something.

When Ginny picked me up in the golf cart, she asked me a ton of questions during the drive to the hotel. I managed to fill her in on most of it. I didn't want her to worry unnecessarily, so I omitted some parts, like Todd trying to attack me.

"Okay, tell me more about this thing with Daniel." She smacked me in the arm. "I can't believe you kept it to yourself. I want details."

"Not much to tell. He's sweet, and I like him."

"Tell me again about kissing him. Were there tongues involved?"

I laughed. "I'd rather not say."

Once at the hotel, I made my way to the Frontenac Suite to return Duchess and drop off the stuff from the pharmacy.

"You were gone more than an hour," Mrs. Garfinkel said the moment she opened the door. She didn't look too pleased.

"I know. I apologize. We had a bit of a detour." Duchess happily trotted inside, then found her bed and promptly curled up and closed her eyes. "She did a lot of running, but she made a little dog friend named Lulu," I explained coyly.

She eyed me for a moment and then glanced down at Duchess, already snoozing. "Are you able to take her out a couple times a week?"

I smiled. "I'll make sure to put it on my schedule."

"Excellent." She handed me an envelope and closed the door.

I fully admit to peeking inside the envelope the second I was alone. There were a few hundreds inside. A contribution to my "moving into an apartment" fund. Which reminded me that I needed to talk to Samuel Park about my job security.

I marched to the office and knocked. I could hear Lois talking. I knocked again, and she opened the door.

"I'm sorry if I'm interrupting." I peered inside the office and saw that she was alone. "Were you on the phone?"

"No. Why?"

"I thought I heard you talking to someone," I replied, hesitant to confront her now that she'd denied the phone conversation.

"I was talking to Henry about the Flower Festival. The festival was always his favorite event of the season," she said, as if discussing things with her dead husband's ghost was as normal as talking to anyone else. Which, for her, it was. The rest of the Park family was worried about her sanity because of that very thing, but Lois didn't seem to care. She was the sole owner of the Park Hotel now, and she let them all know she would do precisely as she pleased.

I was too tired to take on that particular issue at the moment, so I nodded and backed off. "No reason. I'm looking for Samuel."

"I'm pretty sure he's out on the golf course with Casey again."

"Thanks."

I was about to leave when Lois said, "Good work with Mrs. Garfinkel, Andi. I think she has taken a shine to you. Henry's really pleased."

Not quite sure how to respond to praise from a ghost, I simply said, "Uh, thanks. I like her, too. She has spunk."

Lois smiled, "She said the same thing about you."

I left Lois and went to the golf course. I should've waited for Samuel to finish his game and come back to the hotel. But I wasn't feeling very complacent right now. I was determined. Spunky, even.

After inquiring at the clubhouse about Samuel's tee time, I jumped into a cart and set out on the course. Estimating the time for two men to play a hole, I raced the cart toward the ninth hole. I found them just about to tee off on ten.

"Andi, what are you doing here?" Samuel asked. "Is there an emergency at the hotel?"

"No, nothing like that." I glanced over at Casey, who was casually leaning on his club, looking quite smug and satisfied for some reason. "I know this is a bit unorthodox, but I need to talk to you about my position at the hotel."

He frowned. "What about it?"

"I'm planning to rent a place in the village so I can have my cats with me, but I need to know that I won't be looking for another job." I glanced at Casey with a slightly raised eyebrow.

Samuel nodded, realizing what I was hinting at. "Honestly, Andi, I wasn't happy when Lois took you on. And then all the trouble that ensued practically the minute you arrived and hasn't let up. But Lois wanted to help Ginny because you're friends and you were in a pickle."

I opened my mouth to argue my worth, but his look cut me off.

"You've proven yourself. The staff likes you, the guests like you. You have the potential to be a concierge worthy of the Park Hotel."

Puffing out my chest, I smiled at the backhanded compliment. "Thank you."

"Don't get too excited. The fact is that Casey has only been on a leave of absence. His job is promised to him when he's ready to come back to work."

My face fell, and Casey's lit up. He'd been eavesdropping on what we were discussing. He walked over to join us.

"It's really too bad," Samuel continued, "that we can't have two concierges at the hotel. Just seems like that might be excessive. We really only have a need for one, I think."

Casey clapped Samuel on the back. "I have an idea! Andi and I could play this hole for the job." He laughed. "Longest drive wins."

Samuel chuckled along with him.

Ha ha ha.

"Okay," I said as I drew out a club from Samuel's set. "You're on."

Casey made a face. "I was only joking."

"I'm not. Do you want to go first, or shall I?"

He looked at Samuel, who shrugged. "I'll go."

He marched to the tee, set his pretty little ball on top, and then positioned himself. He had good form, and for a second, I questioned my decision. Then he swung. The crack of the club hitting the ball echoed around us. The ball tore through the air and landed on the green. Which would have been great if we were playing the hole. But we weren't.

Casey gave me a satisfied smile and gestured to the tee. "Your turn."

I marched over, put my ball down, set up, and swung a perfect arc. I didn't even have to watch my ball soar to know that I'd hit farther. I saw the stunned looks on Casey and Samuel's faces, which was more than enough confirmation for me.

I handed the club back to Samuel. "I'll see you back at the hotel."

When I jumped into my cart, Casey was already blustering, "We weren't really playing for the job, right, Sam? Just a joke, that's all."

Samuel frowned and shook his head. "I'm sorry, Casey. But a bet is a bet."

"What? You can't be serious," Casey sputtered.

"I'm old-fashioned, son. I come from a time when a man's word means something. I'm sure you already know that," Samuel replied.

"Yes, of course, but—"

"I promised you we'd hold your job open, but you took that promise and stomped on it," Samuel said. "I'm sorry. Maybe we can figure out something else when you're ready to come back to work."

I drove away before I could hear any more of Casey's pleading. When I turned the corner out of sight, I fist-pumped the air and shouted, "Yes!" which became a full-blown cackle of joy. The kind of joy I hadn't felt in a long, long time.

The job was mine. No more worrying about Casey. No more tip-toeing around Samuel, either. Samuel believed I was good at my job. He'd keep me on even when Casey came back. Man, that all felt good. All because I'd hit a golf ball farther than the insufferable Casey Cushing.

Of course, just because Samuel agreed I could keep the job now didn't mean my place was secure forever. Samuel liked Casey, no question about that. He'd be looking for reasons to push me aside. All I had to do was not give him an opening. I could do that. Couldn't I?

By the time I got the golf cart parked and headed toward the hotel, I was already feeling bad about Casey losing his livelihood. Interesting possibility about two concierges, though. Surely that could work. I would call other high-end hotels to see how we could do it. We were definitely busy enough in the summer to justify it. If we shared the job, I could breathe a little easier, too.

I turned the cart around and retraced the path to the tenth hole. I parked on the path and walked toward where Samuel and Casey were talking on the fairway. They both looked up, surprised to see me again so soon no doubt.

"What now, Andi?" Casey said.

I ignored him and spoke to Samuel instead. "I was thinking about the two concierges idea. I think we could make that work, if you're both willing."

Casey's mouth fell open. "You'd be open to that?"

"Sure. This job is not easy. Lots of times, I could use some help. Couldn't you?"

"Well, uh…"

"I'm not sure it would work, but I love that answer, Andi." Samuel's lips widened into a grin that lit up his whole face. "Casey's always been like a grandson to me. There's really nowhere else he might be a good fit at the Park. This kills two birds with one stone. Although maybe I shouldn't use the word 'kill' around you, Andi."

We all got a good laugh out of that one until I said, "Okay. It's settled then. I'll do some research to find out how this might work. And we can talk about it more later. We're holding up the speed of play for those guys behind you."

"Thanks, Andi," Casey said toward my back as I left the fairway and returned to the golf cart. I gave him a little wave in response without turning around.

I parked the cart again and walked toward my suite. My phone vibrated inside my purse. I took it out, smacking myself when I remembered that I had put it on silent. It was the third call from Daniel.

"Hey," I said.

"You do know how to keep a guy on his toes, I'll give you that."

I laughed. "I'm so sorry."

"What was going on?"

"Well, you know that guy we followed to the pawn shop?"

"Am I going to want to hear the rest of this story?"

"Probably not." I chuckled. "But the good news is, I solved the crime and didn't get hurt in the process."

"I bet Sheriff Jackson was happy about that."

I frowned. "The solving part, or the not getting hurt part?"

"The solving part." He was silent for a moment and then continued. "But I'm sure he was happy that you weren't hurt, either."

"Right. Yes."

For the next few minutes, we chatted about seeing each other again and finding the time to do that. We both had busy schedules, but Daniel promised to call me later to figure out when we were both free, and he could either come over to the island or I could go to the mainland.

When I reached my suite, I was feeling content. Tired, but content. I planned to pour myself a glass of wine, run a bath, and relax for a couple of hours. Maybe I'd even read in the bathtub. Except last time I did that, I dropped the book into the water. So maybe I'd wait until I was out of the bath to read.

I kicked off my shoes in the small foyer and decided to check in with the sheriff to make sure everything had gone as planned with Todd and Hannah.

I dug out my phone and dialed the number.

"Why are you calling me Andi? You couldn't possibly have gotten into trouble already. You just left an hour ago."

"No, no trouble. Just wanted to see if everything went okay."

"I know how to do my job."

"Sheriff, relax. Not everything is a critique about your job or how you do it. I just wanted…" I sighed and pulled my hair out of my ponytail. My scalp ached. "I don't know what I wanted, to be honest. Sorry to have bothered you."

"Hannah admitted pushing Mrs. Walker down the stairs on the record. She claims it was an accident, self-defense. Todd was a witness to the event. He confirms her story. And I'm leaning toward believing her. She's pretty bruised up. We'll take pictures and compare them to Mrs. Walker's cane, but it looks like the old woman beat on her pretty good," the Sheriff replied.

"I think maybe Mrs. Walker came upon Hannah stealing something of hers upstairs, and she reacted. From what I've learned, she wasn't a very nice woman, though I wouldn't be too thrilled to find out someone was stealing from me, either. She probably hit that girl as hard as she could, and Hannah pushed her away in defense," I said.

"Yeah, that's my thinking as well."

"What will happen to them, do you think?" I pulled at a thread on my pants. I wasn't feeling all that content anymore.

"They'll serve time for the thefts, for sure. Maybe for the drug dealing, too. Todd has a prior conviction. Hannah's record is clean, so if she gets a good lawyer, she might get away with a couple of years."

I asked, "And what about Colleen?"

"Colleen was there after Todd, but she didn't go into the house far enough to see the body. Too bad, in a way. Might have solved the case a lot sooner," he replied.

I shook my head. I knew justice would be served, but sometimes it just didn't feel all that righteous.

"Thanks, Sheriff."

"Hey, Andi?"

"Yeah?"

"Don't stumble over any more bodies, okay? I haven't had a day off since you arrived on the island."

I chuckled. "I'll try not to."

After we hung up, I got up and went to the balcony windows and looked out at the view. It was so beautiful here. I was blessed to have been able to move here and work. Not everyone was so lucky. This got me thinking about Peter. I felt like he was a victim in all this, and I wondered how, if at all, I could help him. I'd make some calls tomorrow.

But now...now it was time for me to relax.

I walked into the bathroom and started filling the tub with hot water. I'd add a little lavender for scent. Before I could strip off my clothes and get my robe on, there was a knock at the door. I really hoped it wasn't Samuel or Lois wondering if I could do them just one more tiny favor for the hotel. I was "favored" out.

I opened the door to find Lane standing there with another stunning bouquet of flowers. "These came for you." Without waiting for an invitation, he brought them in and settled them on my coffee table. It was a similar arrangement as before.

"Did you see who delivered them?"

He thought for a moment and then frowned. "No, actually, I didn't. They were at the front counter with your name on the delivery sheet."

I don't know why, but my hands shook as I reached for the little white card nestled in the pink and purple flowers. I opened the tiny envelope that had my name scrolled in cursive across it. I pulled out the card, and my hand began to shake as I read it.

See you soon, Andi.

Love, Jeremy

ABOUT THE AUTHOR

Diane Capri is an award-winning *New York Times*, *USA Today*, and world-wide bestselling author. She writes several series, including the Park Hotel Mysteries, the Hunt for Justice, Hunt for Jack Reacher, and Heir Hunter series, and the Jess Kimball Thrillers. She's a recovering lawyer and snowbird who divides her time between Florida and Michigan. An active member of Mystery Writers of America, Author's Guild, International Thriller Writers, Alliance of Independent Authors, and Sisters in Crime, she loves to hear from readers and is hard at work on her next novel.

Please connect with her online:

http://www.DianeCapri.com

Twitter: http://twitter.com/@DianeCapri

Facebook: http://www.facebook.com/Diane.Capri1

http://www.facebook.com/DianeCapriBooks